VAL
LA...

BY
KERRY ALLYNE

MILLS & BOON LIMITED
15–16 BROOK'S MEWS
LONDON WIA IDR

First published 1982
Australian copyright 1982
Philippine copyright 1982
This edition 1982

© Kerry Allyne 1982

ISBN 0 263 73819 1

Set in Monophoto Plantin 10 on 11½ pt.
01/06/82 – 49275

Made and printed in Great Britain by
Richard Clay (The Chaucer Press) Ltd,
Bungay, Suffolk

CHAPTER ONE

'DARLING, guess what's happened! I just had to ring immediately and let you know!' Therese Weldon's happy voice came winging excitedly through the telephone receiver to her daughter, Gayna.

'You've managed to sign up the properties you want to accept visitors for your Homestead-cum-Wildlife Tours,' Gayna guessed, since that had been the project mentioned in her mother's last telephone call from the Northern Territory where she had gone to attend a travel agents' conference.

The Top End, as the northern regions of the Australia continent were popularly called, was booming as a tourist venue, and although her mother's agency was some two and a half thousand kilometres by air to the south in Adelaide, Therese Weldon hadn't managed to develop it into the extremely successful business it was today without being innovative. She seemed to know instinctively what would appeal to the tourist, and although Gayna had often accused her of being too impulsive in putting her ideas into action, at the same time she had to admit that, in business at least, her mother's impetuosity had always paid off. And handsomely, in most cases.

However, on this occasion it appeared business wasn't the reason for her mother's call, because there was quite a lengthy pause before Therese replied, and when she did it was with a rather surprised-sounding,

'Oh! Oh, no, that has nothing to do with it. Well,

only slightly,' she promptly amended with a laugh, her tone becoming enlivened again. 'No, it's something far more thrilling than that, and you'll absolutely never guess.'

Gayna's finely marked brows drew downwards. More thrilling than business? For the last seventeen years—since her father had callously abandoned them—nothing had been more stimulating to her mother than the rearing of a daughter and the success of the agency.

'Perhaps you'd better just tell me what it is, then,' she suggested, her interest piqued.

Her mother laughed delightedly. 'I've met the most gorgeous man and I'm going to get married again!'

'You're *what*?' Gayna came upright on the edge of her chair and sent a horrified look towards the other occupant of the room, her mother's assistant, Alwyn Carson. His return gaze was enquiring and putting her fingers over the mouthpiece she croaked, 'Mum says she's planning to marry again!' A statement which also had his eyes widening in shock and his slight form losing its relaxed attitude.

'His name is Lachlan Montgomery and he has a cattle station south of Darwin,' Therese continued as if her daughter hadn't spoken. 'As a matter of fact, it was his property Clarrie Oliver—one of the other agents I met up here, and who's a friend of Lachlan's—brought me out to. To see for myself the type of activities that would be of interest to visitors.' She gave another chuckle. 'That's what I meant when I said it only slightly had something to do with business.'

'But—but you can't possibly be thinking of marriage!' Gayna stammered, still trying to recover her wits. 'How long have you known him? Three . . . four days? It would be ridiculous to decide to marry someone on such short notice. And—and in any case, I thought you said you'd learnt your lesson last time! You always swore you'd never get caught again!'

'I know I did, darling, but Lachlan's a different type altogether from Everett. You could never call him irresponsible, or unreliable.'

'He's a man, isn't he?' sardonically. Her father's desertion hadn't left Gayna with a particularly favourabele view of the male sex.

'As for the length of time I've known him,' once again Therese went on as if there had been no interruption, 'well, it's closer to two weeks now, actually, but you know me ... I always make my decisions quickly.' An amused male voice sounded in the background and then she spoke again. 'Oh dear, I'm sorry, darling, Lachlan says I'm not giving you the opportunity to say anything because I'm on transmit most of the time and keep forgetting to switch over so I can receive. I'm using a radio telephone, you see, and I'm afraid I'm not very proficient at it at the moment. Have you been trying to talk to me and thought I was ignoring you?'

'Only a couple of times,' Gayna dismissed the instances offhandedly, more interested in returning to the heart of the matter. 'But talking of rapid decisions, I gather Lachlan,' with a rather caustic inflection, 'likes to work that way too, does he, if he's already proposed to you?'

'I guess he must.' It was possible to hear the smile in her mother's voice even if she couldn't see it on her face.

Gayna drew in a deep breath. 'And was that before or *after* he learned you weren't exactly a pauper?'

Momentarily, there was complete silence on the line and then Therese answered more than a little tartly herself. 'Meaning, that's the only reason you think a man would be interested in me?'

'No, of course not!' Gayna protested in dismay. That was the last thing she had intended to imply. After all, no one knew better than she that at forty-two her mother was still a very attractive, and personable, woman. 'I just meant that—that . . .'

'I should question Lachlan's motives in proposing?' Therese cut in.

'Well, that's not so unreasonable, surely, when you've only known him for such a short time?' Gayna felt free to counter, knowing she had her mother's best interests at heart. 'I mean, just how much can you learn about a person in a couple of weeks? You didn't know my father for very long either before you married him, and look how many facets there were to his character— or lack thereof—that you didn't know about.'

'In which case, you might at least give me credit for having grown more astute as I've grown older. I thought you'd be happy for me,' Therese sighed.

Gayna shrugged helplessly, but when Alwyn moved to relieve her of the phone she waved him away with a peremptory gesture. He could add his arguments to hers later. 'I probably would be happy for you if I wasn't so worried you might be making a mistake,' she tried assuaging her mother's obviously hurt feelings. 'I mean, you can't really be positive of his reasons, can you?'

'Can't I?' Therese's tone was dry. 'I'm not a young impressionable girl infatuated with the idea of being in love, you know, Gayna. I do still have my wits about me, and although my decision may seem somewhat precipitate to you, I can assure you I didn't make it lightly.'

Somewhat precipitate? If it hadn't been so serious Gayna would have laughed. She reverted to her original approach. 'But you've been so adamant all these years since you obtained your divorce that wild horses wouldn't be able to drag you to the altar again! What makes this man so different from any of the others who've proposed?' There had been at least three that she knew of.

'Well, for a start, I happen to have fallen in love with Lachlan.'

'You also thought you were with my father,' Gayna reminded her hastily, but only to discover her mother was still transmitting.

'And also because of the type of person he is,' Therese continued. 'From the moment we met it was unbelievable how in tune we were with each other.'

'In other words, he's a smooth-talker as well as everything else, is he?' This time both Gayna's words and her sardonic accents got through.

'No, he is not!' came the emphatic denial in a distinctly cooling voice. 'And if that's the only kind of belittling comment you feel capable of making . . .' For the second time Gayna could hear a voice in the background, and then her mother was advising, 'Lachlan has just suggested you come up here yourself for a visit, to enable you to meet the family and to set your mind at rest, as it were. Under the circumstances I consider it very obliging of him, don't you?'

Gayna didn't immediately say, but queried instead, 'You mean, he's been able to hear everything I've said?' Actually, she thought that might perhaps have been just as well, except she was sorry if it had embarrassed her mother, but at least it let Lachlan Montgomery know she wasn't about to be won over as easily as her parent apparently had been.

'Not exactly—only my answers—but they were obviously sufficient to give him the gist of the conversation,' drily.

'So he's a widower, is he?' The reference to meeting the family suddenly flashed back into Gayna's mind. 'With a large family?' she asked innocently.

'Darling, he doesn't need a stepmother for his children, if that's what you're now trying to imply,' Therese replied in a half humorous, half exasperated tone. 'He only has two and they're both older than you are. Now, are you going to accept his offer and come for a visit or not?'

Naturally she was! At closer quarters not only would she be able to study the man for herself more closely, but it would also be easier to dissuade her mother from going ahead with such a rash, and rushed, marriage.

'Oh, yes, I'll come,' she advised pungently. 'I'll catch the plane to Darwin the day after tomorrow. Then how do I get to wherever you are from there?'

There was a slight pause and then Therese came back on the line. 'Lachlan says he'll send someone to meet you at the airport. That will be easier than you trying to arrange transport out to Mundamunda.'

'Is that the name of the property, or the nearest town?' Gayna enquired, momentarily sidetracked.

'The property,' was her mother's laughing reply. 'There is no town. Well, not for quite some distance, anyway.'

'I see.' Gayna's expression turned wry. The outback had never particularly appealed to her—she preferred the conveniences of the city—but in this instance she didn't have a choice in the matter. She was about to head into the Never-Never, like it or not! 'Well, I guess I'll see you the day after tomorrow, then.' Catching sight of a movement from the corner of her eye, she hurried on, 'Oh, before you go, Alwyn's here with me and I think he'd like a word with you too.'

'Mmm, and I can imagine what about! No, I think I'll give it a miss for this evening. Tell him to ring me on this number,' detailing it so Gayna could make a note, 'tomorrow morning and I'll speak to him then. I've got a few notes I want to pass on to him about the business in any case, but I don't happen to have them to hand just at the moment.'

'Okay, I'll tell him.'

'And I'll look forward to seeing you shortly, darling. I think you're going to be pleasantly surprised, you know.'

Gayna seriously doubted it but refrained from saying so—at least to her mother—but when their goodbyes had been said and the receiver replaced in its cradle, she was far more outspoken with her mother's assistant.

'I can't believe it!' she exclaimed, riffling her fingers through the shining cap of her auburn hair. 'I know Mum usually acts on impulse, but this—this is absolutely ridiculous! To even remotely consider getting married when she's only known him for just over a week ... why, it's incredible! I think the heat must have got to her.'

'Or someone else has,' put in Alwyn darkly, his thin features tightening. At twenty-nine he had been with the Weldon agency for six years now and his position as Therese's assistant had often entailed him becoming involved in their family matters, so that he felt no qualms now in discussing his employer's intended marriage. 'You should have let me speak to her as well,' he added censoriously. 'She probably would have paid more attention to any arguments I might have offered.'

'I don't see why,' Gayna retorted, nettled. Alwyn always thought he knew better than anyone else. 'Anyway, I tried to get her to speak to you, but she said for you to ring her at this number in the morning.' Tearing off the top sheet of the pad she had used to make her notation, she handed it across to him. 'You'll be able to see how effective your arguments are then.'

Taking the piece of paper from her, he eyed it cursorily, then folded it and inserted it in his wallet. 'While you're planning to fly up there the day after tomorrow, I take it?' he sought confirmation with a questioning frown.

'You bet I am!' she nodded emphatically. 'Goodness only knows what sweet nothings he's used to sweep Mum off her feet, but he won't find it so easy to pull the wool over my eyes.'

'I'll go with you!'

Those selfsame darkly lashed, grey-green eyes now rounded in surprise. 'Where . . . to Mundamunda? But you can't,' she vetoed promptly. 'Someone has to stay here to take charge of the agency, and especially since Cliff's away at present too.'

'Damn! I'd forgotten he's off sick.' His lips pursed thoughtfully. 'Although it shouldn't be long before he's back, should it?'

Gayna shrugged noncommittally. 'Who knows with these weird viruses? Some of them can put you to bed for weeks.'

Besides, now that she knew the direction of Alwyn's thought she hoped Cliff didn't rush back to work. His attitude towards her had become too proprietorial for her liking of late. Everywhere she went, Alwyn found a reason to go too. Like this evening, for example. She hadn't really wanted his escort home after working late, but he had determinedly overridden her wishes anyway.

'In any case, I don't really think there's a need for both of us to go, even if we had both been *invited*,' she stressed pointedly. 'It's not a show of strength that's wanted, but the power of reasoning.'

'Perhaps,' he acceded, but with patent reluctance. 'Although I hardly think I require an invitation to visit the area. I could always stay at the nearest town, if necessary.'

'Except that there apparently doesn't happen to be one—at least, not for quite some distance—and you know how much you'd hate it being stuck out in the middle of nowhere.' Alwyn was even more of a city dweller at heart than she was!

The corners of his mouth turned down in a disgruntled fashion. 'Then I suppose I have no option but to wait until Therese decides to return to Adelaide, have I?' he heaved grudgingly. 'How much longer does she expect to stay at this place? Did she say?'

'As a matter of fact she didn't,' Gayna shook her head disappointedly. 'But you can rest assured I'll be doing my utmost to see that it's as short as possible. The quicker she's away from this man's influence the better, as far as I can see!'

'Hmm, and in the meantime, maybe it wouldn't go amiss if I were to do some checking on him. You never know what I might manage to uncover.'

'That's a good idea,' Gayna agreed, willing to be a little more helpful now that he seemed resigned to not accompanying her. 'His name is Lachlan Montgomery, and the property's called Mundamunda. You already have the telephone number, so if you did come across anything worth passing on, you could always ring me.'

'I'll certainly do that,' he nodded, and began easing himself to his feet, a possessive light entering his pale brown eyes as they appraised her slender form.

Seeing it, Gayna surmised he was about to make another of his unencouraged attempts to monopolise her company for the remainder of the evening, and sprang to her own feet with the hopefully forestalling suggestion, 'You're off then, are you? I'll see you to the door.'

Unfortunately, however, Alwyn wasn't that easily rebuffed. 'As a matter of fact, since neither of us has eaten yet, I was about to recommend we go somewhere for dinner together,' he announced, totally unperturbed.

If it had been anyone else, Gayna would have given an outright refusal and left it at that, but in Alwyn's case the circumstances were somewhat different. Not only was he her mother's second-in-command, but she herself had to work with him at the agency every day, so in order to avoid any disharmony in the office she had to be a little more restrained with her rejections. A fact, she suspected with annoyance, Alwyn played on to a very large degree.

Now, with an inward grimace, she gave a declining shake of her head but accompanied it with an apologetic smile. 'Thank you for the thought, but not tonight, Alwyn, if you don't mind. What with all this business concerning Mum, I don't really feel I would be very good company, and if I'm off to Darwin shortly I think I'd better see about organising some summer clothes to take with me.' She indicated the tailored woollen suit and silk blouse she was wearing. 'Somehow, I don't think this type of outfit will be terribly suitable for spring in the tropics.'

'You still have to eat,' he persisted.

'I'll just fix myself something light here at home. An omelette, or something similar.'

'That's not exactly what I would call a sustaining meal.'

'But sufficient, all the same,' she declared.

'Perhaps if I stayed and helped you, we would put together something more filling,' he now put forward, ignoring her increasingly clipped tone.

Gayna inhaled deeply and drew herself up to her full five feet one. 'I don't *want* anything more filling, thank you, Alwyn!' And taking a couple of determined steps towards the door, 'Now, I'm sorry, but I really will have to ask you to excuse me. I have a lot I want to get done this evening.'

His lips thinned angrily. 'Then we'll make it tomorrow night,' he stated arrogantly. 'I'll reserve a table for us at his new little restaurant I've found. You'll like it there.'

'That's as may be,' she allowed, but not without some sarcasm as her temper flared. 'But I happen to have already made arrangements for tomorrow night, so I'm afraid I won't be going with you.'

His eyes narrowed suspiciously. 'What other arrangements?'

'*Private* arrangements!' she snapped acidly. 'I take it you have no objection?'

'With a man?'

'You're over-stepping yourself, Alwyn! That's my business, not yours!' How dared he presume to interrogate her!

A muscle jerked angrily at the side of his jaw. 'I'm sorry,' he muttered stiffly, but without the least sound of remorse in his tone. 'I merely thought it would make better use of the evening if we took the opportunity to discuss what you should say to Therese when you see her.'

'Oh?' Gayna's brows arched sardonically. 'You don't believe I'm capable of deciding that for myself?'

'I thought you'd be pleased to have my help.'

'I am,' she conceded sincerely. 'But at the same time, it is *my* mother we're talking about and I think I know her a little better than you do.'

'I don't agree,' he countered promptly. 'When you work with someone for as long as I have with Therese, you get to know them fairly thoroughly, and I'm of the opinion that logic will have more of an effect on her than emotional entreaties.'

A whimsical curve tilted Gayna's mouth upwards. 'And just what makes you think I'm planning to resort to—er—emotional entreaties, as you call them?'

'You won't be able to help yourself,' he predicted in his most patronising manner. 'Women never can in a crisis.'

'Well, this one can, believe me!' Her swift retort was confidently voiced. And especially where men and marriage were concerned, she added silently to herself. Her impulsive mother might have foolishly relaxed her guard and allowed her heart to temporarily rule her head, but Gayna had never experienced any such difficulty in her relationships with the opposite sex, and she wasn't about to let her feelings take charge now when the outcome was so important. No matter how charming Lachlan Montgomery might try to be! 'I can be as controlled and calculating as any man if the occasion warrants it,' she added forcefully to ensure there were no doubts left in his mind.

'Let's hope so, then, for both our sakes!'

'Both our sakes?' she repeated, frowning. Now that she came to think of it, just why was Alwyn so concerned that her mother might marry again? After all, it wasn't as if he had a personal interest in the matter like she did.

'Mmm, you're not the only one who'll be effected by this marriage if it takes place, you know,' he enlightened her crisply. 'I've more or less had a verbal agreement with Therese for some time now, that if she should ever decide to sell the agency she'll give me the first option to purchase.'

It didn't really surprise her. She had always known he was keen to go into business for himself, but she still couldn't quite see why the present turn of events should worry him so much.

'And?' she prompted, a little perplexed.

'At the moment I wouldn't have a hope in hell of raising the necessary money.'

'Then I doubt Mum would sell until you did have,' she assured him.

Alwyn didn't look very convinced. 'She might not want to, but would her new husband?' he returned sardonically. 'He could have entirely different ideas. And not only that, but if the agency was sold, all our jobs—*yours* included—could then depend upon the new owner. Have you thought of that?'

As it so happened, she hadn't. 'But even if Mum did marry him, the agency would still belong to her. He couldn't force her to sell it if she didn't want to, and I'm positive she . . .'

'Oh, Gayna, don't be so naïve,' he cut in pityingly.

'If this chap's got her so infatuated she's talking of marriage already, there's no telling what he could persuade her to do if they should actually proceed to the altar!'

It wasn't an aspect she had foreseen—until then her main concerns had been of a purely personal nature—but now that Alwyn had raised the matter, it became just one more reason for her to inject some caution into her mother's impetuous thinking.

CHAPTER TWO

IT was the middle of the afternoon when Gayna arrived in Darwin, and no sooner had she left the plane and walked across the tarmac to the airport terminal than she stripped off the heavy-knit cardigan she had been wearing over her denim skirt and long-sleeved blouse, and draped it between the handles of the large carryall she had brought with her. The temperature in the northern capital was at least double what it had been in Adelaide when she left that morning, and already she was eagerly anticipating the end of her journey—if only so she could change into something a little cooler.

Inside the not particularly large building there was the usual flurry of activity associated with new arrivals and impending departures to be found at most airports. People being greeted, others saying farewell. Some making last-minute purchases from the shop, while still others either sought, or directed, porters with their luggage. Overhead, the public address system was almost continually giving flight announcements, making final calls for latecomers, and notifying individuals that they were required either on the telephone or at the information desk.

Gayna listened to these latter messages intently, expecting to hear her own name called at any moment. But as the minutes wore on and the general bustle began to diminish as increasing numbers of her fellow passengers departed, and those who had already been waiting headed for their respective planes—mostly charters or private craft, she noted—it became obvious that whoever was being sent to meet her had either been held up somewhere or hadn't bothered to be punctual, and she looked about her with mounting impatience. After a long flight, and with still more travelling to do before she finally reached her destination, she had expected to be met immediately, not to have to stand around waiting in this unaccustomed heat!

In order to, she hoped, save time later, she collected her luggage and carried it across to a seat near the information desk where she sat down and lit a cigarette, her eyes glancing over those people remaining in the building as she did so. Although some were apparently on their own, as she was, most seemed to be in groups of two or three—a large percentage of them Aboriginals returning to mission stations, and the like—and, presumably, most of them passengers for the many small planes still parked close to the runway.

Presently, the glass doors which led out on to the tarmac swung open to admit the tall, wide-shouldered figure of a man dressed in the usual close-fitting jeans and check shirt of a bushman who, after one cursory look over the other occupants of the building, had his attention claimed by three drill-clad men not far distant. For some unaccountable reason—perhaps merely because she had nothing else to do—Gayna found herself continuing to watch the foursome contemplatively.

From her first survey she had already mentally decided that the three in drill were graziers, but the status of this latest addition to their little group was somewhat harder to define. Admittedly, his was the most commanding figure, but then that might only have been because he was tallest, as well as the young-

est and more muscular of the group. She surmised he
was in his early thirties, whereas his companions were
all one side or the other of fifty. Speculating finally
that he was probably just an employee of some kind,
and more than likely of one of the men with whom he
was conversing, she directed her gaze elsewhere. A
burst of highly amused laughter some short time later
had her eyes promptly swinging back their way again,
however, and involuntarily resuming their idle ap-
praisal.

A young girl of some eighteen years had joined the
group now, her expression rapt due to holding the tallest man's smiling attention, and as Gayna took stock
of his crisply curling dark hair and ruggedly good-
looking features, she felt an uncontrollable surge of
dislike well up inside her.

From her mother's description, Everett Weldon, her
father, had been just such a man. Handsome, accepting
women's admiration as a matter of course ... and
totally selfish and undependable as a result! Gayna
pressed her lips together in disgust. Good grief, didn't
the girl realise she was only making a spectacle of
herself gazing up at him in such a fashion when it
was perfectly obvious—even to a stranger like herself—that the man didn't reciprocate her feelings in
the slightest?

Looking away quickly, she stubbed out her cigarette
with an irritable movement and then gave a brief, tight
smile of self-satisfaction. At least she could be thankful
that she was never likely to be taken in by such types.
In fact, it had always afforded her some considerable
pleasure to be able to turn the tables on them instead
and deflate their insufferable egos whenever she was
given the opportunity. A practice, she unworriedly

recalled her mother forecasting, which would rebound
on her some day.

'Gayna Weldon?'

The rather curtly spoken enquiry brought her out of
her reverie with a slight start, but that was nothing
compared to the shock she received when, on looking
up, she discovered herself confronting the very same
man who had been the object of her disparaging
thoughts such a short time before.

'Y—yes,' she acknowledged, stammering, and
furious with herself for not only sounding so path-
etically disconcerted, but for inconsequentially noting
that his eyes were a deep blue when she had expected
them to be brown because of his dark colouring.

He hefted her suitcase into one hand as if it weighed
no more than a pound or two—which it certainly did!—
and took a pace back in the direction he had come
from. 'Shall we go?'

'Go?' she echoed a little distractedly, gaining her
own feet. 'Go where? And—and just who are you,
anyway?'

'The name's Ford,' he supplied in the same terse
tone, but with a hint of impatience in it now as well.
'As for where to . . . well, Mundamunda, of course.'
One dark eyebrow slanted upwards, openly sarcastic.
'Or are you having second thoughts?'

Gayna contemptuously ignored the last, but gasped
angrily, 'You mean, *you're* the person who was
supposed to meet me when I arrived?'

'Haven't I?' he shrugged unconcernedly.

'Only when it suited you, apparently!' she flared.
'You've been here for at least thirty minutes!'

'So?' he challenged coldly.

She could hardly believe her ears. 'So you might

have had the decency to let me know immediately, instead of leaving me sitting here in this heat wondering if I was going to be met, after all, while you stood around casually chit-chatting to all and sundry! Somehow I doubt that was quite what your employer had in mind when he sent you in here, Mr Ford!'

For a moment his dark blue eyes held a savage light and then he flexed his broad shoulders dismissively. 'It's not Mr—Just Ford'll do,' he corrected as he recommenced walking.

With no other choice left to her, Gayna had, perforce, to follow him, her thoughts no less aggravated and confused than they had been at the beginning. 'Well, we're going in the wrong direction, in any case, aren't we? The road's that way.' She flung out a hand behind her to indicate the front of the building.

'Except that they don't allow planes to take off from there.' His retort was mockingly made.

'We're flying to Mundamunda?' She couldn't keep the surprise out of her voice.

The scornful look he sent her made her feel like a stupid child. 'How did you think we were going to get there . . . by walking?'

'No, by car, of course!' she snapped back infuriatedly. Since her mother hadn't seen fit to mention anything about an extra plane trip, naturally she had assumed that was the way they'd be travelling. 'I gather they *do* have roads, even to places like Mundamunda.' She gave vent to a little sarcasm herself.

'But not, once you leave the highway, of the kind you're used to, or that you'd like,' he appeared to take some pleasure in informing her as they passed through the doorway and began heading for the concrete apron where the light planes waited.

The blazing sunlight which greeted them had Gayna digging into her carryall in order to find her sunglasses and to slide them gratefully on to her finely sculptured nose. As her previous assumption that the man beside her was only an employee had been proved correct—even if to the wrong employer—she began looking about her expectantly.

'Where's the pilot, then?' she finally asked when it became apparent no one was preparing to join them.

Again he fixed her with one of those gibing glances that made her blood boil. 'How many do you want?'

It took a while for her to realise just what he was implying. '*You're* a qualified pilot?' she couldn't help questioning to make certain she had understood.

'No, an unqualified one,' he promptly retorted with sardonic overtones.

Gayna's temper soared rapidly. 'Well, I could hardly be expected to know what qualifications you possess, could I?' she defended herself indignantly. 'But although you seem extremely displeased at having been sent to meet me,' what other reason could there be to explain his deliberately rude and offensive behaviour? 'I suggest you don't take out your annoyance on me any further, or I'm afraid I shall be forced to report your disgraceful conduct to your employer when we arrive at the property!' She let him know her feelings on the matter exactly.

Halting beside a six-seater Piper, he opened the door and tossed her suitcase unceremoniously inside, his expression showing no concern whatsoever with regard to her threat. 'Get in,' he merely ordered in bored accents.

After grudgingly having done so, she glanced resolutely down at him. 'I meant what I said,' she declared determinedly lest he should think she had only been bluffing.

'I'm shaking in my boots,' he quipped, shutting the door between them.

While he checked the outside of the aircraft Gayna could only hold her tongue, but as soon as he took his own seat it was impossible for her to control her vexation any longer and she burst out fierily, 'You may feel very confident at the moment, Mr—er—er—Ford, but I shouldn't let it go to your head, if I were you, because I don't make idle threats, believe me!'

'Neither do I, you little shrew, so I wouldn't recommend you rile me into uttering a few of my own!' he ground out ominously, the sheer animosity evident in his eyes taking her breath away. 'So now I suggest you just keep your mouth *shut* and let me get us on our way!' Switching first one and then the other engine on, he began conversing with the control tower.

Gayna was too stunned to say anything—even if she had wanted to. Of all the . . .! Who in hell did he think he was to call her a shrew, when he had been the cause of all the trouble in the first place? If he's just made an effort to be on time instead of standing around talking—as well as lapping up that blonde girl's attention, she added tartly—then probably none of the other would have followed. Although, then again, his attitude hadn't exactly been endearing right from the outset, she reminded herself with some asperity.

It wasn't her fault he'd been given a job he didn't care to undertake . . . and yet the fact that he'd been sent to Darwin hadn't appeared to worry him while he'd been talking with those graziers, and nor did it satisfactorily explain that so incredibly hostile gaze he had just bestowed on her. Okay, so she'd just vowed to put him in to his boss, but as he hadn't shown the least concern when she made the threat, she couldn't quite bring herself to believe that it would suddenly have been the cause of such an openly antagonistic reaction.

As they taxied to the runway she eyed her companion surreptitiously from the cover provided by her sunglasses, two creases of puzzlement making their appearance between her brows as she studied his grimly set profile. No, she eventually decided on a deeply exhaled breath, there *had* to be some other reason for that scarcely veiled antipathy which had been present right `from the first moment he had spoken to her. Immediately they were airborne, and with Darwin fast disappearing behind them, she set about seeking some answers while simultaneously keeping her own displeasure with the situation under tight rein.

'How did you know who I was when you spoke to me in the terminal?' she asked initially, partly as a matter of interest for herself, and partly as a lead up for him.

A chilling blue gaze was all she received for her efforts at first, but then he shrugged impassively. 'I was told to look for a redhead. You were the only one there.'

So far, so good. 'And you did purposely keep me waiting, didn't you?'

This time he didn't even turn his head, let alone answer.

'Why?' she pressed on regardless, taking his silence for affirmation.

Now she got a reply—a derisively grated, 'You really want to know?'

'Y—yes,' she nodded.

'You don't sound very sure.'

'Well, I am!' Gayna's voice rose a little. Lord only knew why, but he seemed to have the power to rattle her more than anyone she had ever known. Clamping down on her emotions again, she probed speculatively, 'It wasn't, by any chance, your employer's . . .'

'For a start, let's get one thing straight,' he interrupted impatiently. 'I don't know what gave you the idea, but I don't *have* an employer!'

Behind the dark circles of her glasses Gayna's eyes narrowed in confusion, even as her cheeks reddened at the thought of her threats to report him. 'Then wh—where *do* you fit in, in all this?' Was he a neighbour, perhaps?

'Snow asked me to collect you.'

'Snow?' she quizzed, more perplexed than ever.

'Lachlan Montgomery to you,' he supplied briefly.

She nodded her understanding. So the man her mother had become involved with was an ash-blond, was he? 'And you weren't very happy about having been asked, I take it,' she deduced ironically.

'Quite frankly, I thought the trip by road would have been no more than your just deserts . . . *if* you had to be invited to the property at all!' His words lashed out at her with scorching clarity.

Startled once again by that sudden show of vehemence, Gayna burst out furiously, 'How—how dare you!' as indignation and anger vied for supremacy. 'What business is it of yours if I'm invited to Mundamunda or not?'

'It's my business because I happen to live there!' she was informed on a harshly roughening note as his eyes raked over her disparagingly. 'And I, for one, feel under no obligation whatsoever to make any effort on behalf of a spoiled, selfish, and utterly obnoxious little

miss who thinks she can make any accusation she
pleases about my family with impunity—no matter
how detestable—solely in an attempt to justify her own
warped way of thinking!'

'Are you t—talking about m—*me*?' she gasped incredulously, and almost choking on her accelerating
emotions.

One of Ford's dark brows lifted sarcastically high.
'You recognise the description, then?'

Words almost failed her—but, luckily, not quite.
'Why, you smug, patronising, insufferable bore! Just
who do you think you are, to lecture me? If I think it's
warranted I'll accuse whoever I like of whatever I like,
and you can go to hell!' She swung towards the window
to stare fixedly at the ground passing below them, her
breasts heaving rapidly with the strength of her feelings. A bare moment later she swivelled back again, a
chance recollection causing her to demand suspiciously, 'And what do you mean, *your* family?'

'It's my father your mother's planning to marry!'
was the completely unanticipated but stony divulgence.

Flames of fury rampaged through Gayna's insides.
Of course, he couldn't have let that little piece of pertinent information slip in the beginning, could he? Oh,
no, he'd carefully refrained from doing that! she remembered. Well, Ford Montgomery was about to discover the battle had only just begun! With due de-
liberation she removed her sunglasses in order to allow
her eyes to travel slowly, depreciatingly, the full length
of him.

'Then she must have been duped even more than I
thought!' she gibed acidly.

The knuckles on his hand nearest her whitened as

his fingers clenched, and the tightening of his expression which accompanied the gesture was enough to have her swallowing apprehensively. 'More evidence of your distorted views on life, hmm?' he jeered just as bitingly.

That was the second time he'd made such a comment. 'Meaning?'

'According to Therese, that just because your father deserted the two of you, you've since managed to convince yourself that all men are tarred with the same brush!'

'Aren't they?' she half smiled bitter-sweetly.

'Where you're concerned, I wouldn't be at all surprised,' he was willing to concede, mockingly. 'They probably find your attitude is merely a front to hide your own frigid nature.'

Gayna's eyes flashed emerald fire and it was only with a great deal of effort that she was able to force her smile into remaining on her lips. 'What a typical male reaction,' she charged sardonically. 'If a woman doesn't immediately fall at your feet, you automatically assume she's frigid. It just doesn't occur to you that some of us can see your shallow posturings for exactly what they really are—ego trips—does it?' She gave a low taunting laugh. 'Well, I'm sorry to disappoint you, but I don't intend making a fool of myself over any man, and if that's distorted thinking in your view, then that's just too bad. At least it's better than waking up one morning to find your loved one has suddenly decided the grass is greener elsewhere!'

'In other words . . . you're frightened!' he asserted scornfully.

Her arched brows flew skywards. 'Of what?'

'Life in general, and men in particular, by the sound

of it!' came the contemptuous retort, followed by, 'You know what your trouble is, don't you?'

'Do tell,' she prompted flippantly.

'You're just plain scared you're not *able* to hold a man's interest!'

'Oh, my God!' Gayna exclaimed in disbelief. 'Your male ego is showing again! You men really do hate to think there's any of us who can resist you, don't you? You'd much rather we were all like your female companion at the airport—hanging on your every word as if our very lives depended upon it.'

He didn't dispute it, but merely asked sardonically instead, 'And is that how you came to be such an authority on the subject? By spying on people?'

'I don't spy—I observe,' she reproved dulcetly. 'Although, of course, *if* I had been met on time, there wouldn't have been the necessity for me to occupy myself doing that either, would there?'

'That still rankles, does it?' he grinned suddenly, and annoyingly reminding her once more just how attractive he was. 'Well, never mind. As I said, if the choice had been mine, I would have left you to make the trip by road.'

'Then it's probably a pity you didn't! At least that way I might have enjoyed the company,' she returned somewhat more tartly. 'As it is, I'm beginning to wish Alwyn had been able to come with me, after all.'

'Alwyn?' He flicked her an interrogating glance. 'Therese's manager?'

'Mmm, he's not very taken with the idea of this proposed marriage either,' she was pleased to report.

A cynical curve swept Ford's mouth downwards. 'So she said after he'd phoned her yesterday. I gather he sees himself as something of a family mentor.'

Knowing Alwyn, he probably did, Gayna granted wryly, but at the same time she could have wished her mother hadn't been quite so generous with her information. Especially regarding herself!

'I'm glad he does think of himself as such,' she lied blatantly. In actual fact, there was no way she wanted Alwyn intruding in her or her mother's personal affairs, but under the present circumstances it could prove an advantage to let the man beside her believe she had no objections. 'Mum isn't averse to accepting his advice either,' she added for good measure.

'No?' Up went those dark brows again in a satirically goading movement. 'She certainly appeared to take exception to it yesterday. Perhaps, unlike you, *she* feels quite capable of trusting her emotions and doesn't require outside interference,' he smiled aggravatingly.

'Then she's obviously forgotten how she would have welcomed it before she married my father!' Gayna rounded on him testily.

'Mmm, but if she had, then you wouldn't be here to remind her of it now, would you?' drily.

'That's irrelevant!' she snapped, irritated. 'I *am* here, even though you quite obviously wish it were otherwise, and I intend to see she does remember.'

'Whether Therese wants to or not?'

'Yes!'

Ford's ensuing intake of breath was short and sharp, his ebony-lashed eyes so piercingly cold as they stabbed at her that she shivered involuntarily. 'You really are a selfishly cold-blooded little bitch, aren't you?' he denounced scathingly. 'You couldn't care less whether your mother was happy, unhappy, or in a state of limbo somewhere in between, could you? No, you with all your petty fears and inhibitions are only concerned with *your* feelings, *your* ideas, *your* wants and needs, with never a thought for anyone else!'

'That's not true! It is my mother I'm thinking of!' Gayna fired back fiercely, resentfully. 'And if you've got nothing to hide, then why all this commotion because I want to be certain my mother's not making a mistake? Answer that one if you can . . . or if you dare!' she threw back at him insolently.

Momentarily, the only sound that could be heard inside the cabin was the rhythmic drone of the plane's engines, then Ford was rasping direfully between gritted teeth, 'If I did, I doubt you'd appreciate . . .'

'In other words, you can't!' she broke in recklessly.

'In other words, don't fall into the trap of thinking your sex gives you automatic immunity from reprisal for every wild and offensive slur you care to spout!' he amended savagely.

'Oh?' she shrugged carelessly, albeit a trifle sulkily. 'Well, I guess that's as good an excuse as any if you want to avoid giving an answer, isn't it?'

'Gayna! Although my father may be prepared to be more forbearing, there's a limit to how much I intend letting you ride *me*, and you've just reached it!' he warned on an explosive note.

Regardless, she still demanded, 'Then why won't you answer?'

'Because I refuse to dignify such an unfounded accusation even to that extent, that's why!' he grated.

She pulled a decidedly disbelieving face. 'Another handy excuse?' she dared to mutter, and found herself on the receiving end of the hardest-eyed, most disdainful stare he had given her yet.

'You can call it what you like, I don't give a damn!' he retaliated squashingly.

He might not now, but once she had spoken to her mother ... well, that could be something else again! she decided silkily, but on this occasion prudently restrained herself from voicing her thoughts aloud. As yet he was still a relatively unknown quantity, and if she did, in fact, go too far, she had no way of telling just what his reaction might be.

Instead, she partly turned her back to him in order to give her full attention to the scenery below them where vast grassy plains merged with paperbark swamps, and winding watercourses were clearly defined by their edgings of dark green growth. Ahead of them, and set nearby one of those life-giving rivers—or creeks, as she supposed they really were—a cluster of silver-roofed buildings eventually became visible and, her curiosity getting the better of her, she cast a glance back over her shoulder to her companion.

'Is that Mundamunda?' she enquired hopefully. Anything would be preferable to continuing their close confinement.

'Yes.' His curt affirmation was accompanied by an even more concise nod.

Surmising that his sentiments echoed hers exactly, Gayna gave a small inward smile of satisfaction. At least she had the pleasure of knowing not everything had gone his way! It also gave her the confidence to ask another question.

'Is it a very large property?' She knew most of them were in the Territory.

'Large enough. Why?'

'I was just wondering,' she both shrugged and frowned.

'Wondering whether we needed your mother's

money to help run it, you mean!' he retorted with extreme sarcasm.

Actually, she hadn't been, but as he had so kindly presented the opportunity, she couldn't help but smile tauntingly, 'Well, do you?'

With unexpected swiftness Ford's hand suddenly caught her chin in an inescapable grip as he leant slightly towards her. 'Sorry—but no, we don't,' he replied in a similarly goading vein. His mocking blue eyes held hers relentlessly. 'Disappointed?'

'Not really,' she offered with assumed indifference, while all the time trying desperately to overcome the vexing awareness she felt at his touch. 'Even if you did, I wouldn't expect you to admit it.'

'So why ask?'

'Why not?' she countered, defensively challenging. 'I had nothing to lose.'

'Just a hell of a lot to learn, huh?'

'That's a matter of opinion!'

The amused laugh which issued from the deeply bronzed column of his throat as he released her in order to return his attention to the controls and begin their descent had Gayna experiencing a mixed emotional reaction. Relief, that he had removed the unaccountably disturbing contact, and a rising resentment at his continual arrogant disparagements.

All right, so she had come up here with the intention of persuading her mother not to marry his father, that still didn't give him the right to treat her in such a contemptuous and cavalier manner, did it? With an impotent glare for the object of her rancorous thoughts she settled back in preparation for their landing.

This was accomplished with an ease born of long practice on a red sandy strip cut from the scrub only a

couple of hundred yards or so distant from the homestead and outbuildings, and once Ford had brought
the aircraft to rest they proceeded to cross the intervening ground on foot.

At first the place gave the appearance of being
deserted as it lay passively in the somnolent late afternoon heat, although Gayna supposed that probably
wasn't so surprising since, no doubt, most of whatever
male staff they had would still be out working, and it
was left to those dogs which had remained behind to
vociferously offer an initial welcome. Continuing on,
they passed numerous structures—some housing
equipment, others obviously living quarters of one
form or another—until at last they came to the fence
encircling the homestead itself and associated gardens.

Once through the gateway the white-painted house
could be seen clearly. Its design was typical of the
colonial tropics, being set a yard or so above the ground
and with wide lattice-decorated verandahs to block the
sun's entry, while two giant spreading Indian raintrees
provided dappled shade for the roof. It was a large,
very gracious-looking building, but Gayna's apprecia-
tion of its aesthetic appeal was rapidly diverted as she
saw four figures emerge on to the front verandah.

One of them she recognised immediately—her
mother—and she naturally presumed the tall blond—
or was it white-headed?—man next to her to be Ford's
father, but the other two were somewhat harder to
pigeonhole. Both female and in their late twenties, one
was petite and dark, the other of medium height and
blonde. Could one be a sister to Ford? Gayna
wondered. She remembered her mother saying there
were two children in the family. But if so, which one?
The brunette whose hair was as dark as Ford's was, or

the blonde whose hair resembled his father's? With a dismissing shrug she decided to let time sort the matter out for her.

'Darling, it's lovely to see you! Did you have a good flight?' It was Therese who spoke first as Gayna and Ford mounted the front steps.

Kissing her mother's smooth cheek in greeting, Gayna was tempted to reply that she could have done without the second leg of it, but judiciously guarded her tongue. 'Very good, thank you,' she murmured politely instead.

'And now you must meet Lachlan,' her mother went on happily, turning her around to face the man beside her whose deep blue eyes were identical to his son's— except that his held no signs of hostility, only a kindly and interested light.

'How do you do, Mr Montgomery.' Gayna proffered her hand when her mother's introduction had been completed.

Accepting it, he shook his head slightly in veto. 'No, please, make it Lachlan as your mother does, or Snow as my children do, if you prefer, but nothing quite so formal as Mr, hmm?' he suggested in a pleasantly modulated voice.

'Thank you,' she nodded, albeit rather selfconsciously. Considering her reason for being there, a more formal atmosphere would have suited her better.

Her mother seemed to be deliberately ignoring that particular aspect, however, she noted, as Therese continued, 'And this is Raeleen—Raeleen Daniels— Lachlan's daughter,' indicating the smaller brunette, 'and this is Felicity Stanbrooke, a friend of Raeleen's,' gesturing towards the blonde this time. There was a brief pause while the three girls exchanged acknowledgements and then she laughed, 'You've already met Ford, of course.'

'Mmm.' Gayna's response wasn't particularly expansive, and nor was the almost grimacing half smile which accompanied it, but it was all she could manage as she kept her lips pressed tightly together to avoid adding the caustic, 'More's the pity!' which was on the verge of following.

'Then might I suggest we all adjourn to the other end of the verandah for some refreshments?' Lachlan Montgomery enquired of them generally. 'I expect Gayna would like something cold to drink after her trip, if nothing else.'

'I'd like to wash and change into something a little cooler first, though, if I may,' Gayna put in hurriedly, and gave her heavyweight clothes a rueful glance. 'I'm afraid it was nowhere near as warm as this in Adelaide when I left.'

'No, I suppose not,' he smiled in understanding, and then at her mother. 'Perhaps you'd care to show her through, Therese? I imagine the two of you would like a chat together, in any case.'

The suggestion was accepted with alacrity, and promising, 'We won't be long,' Therese began ushering Gayna into the wide entrace hall.

From there they made their way past a maple-panelled sitting room and an elegantly appointed dining room before reaching the bedrooms situated on the right of the building, and entered a large and comfortably furnished room decorated in delicate tones of lavender.

Following her mother inside, Gayna gazed cursorily about her, then stopped in surprise on seeing Ford standing in the doorway, her brows peaking enquiringly.

'Your luggage,' he enlightened her wryly, moving into the room with the case which had been out of sight until then. 'Where do you want it?'

'Oh! Oh, at the end of the bed will do, thank you,' she replied, flustered. His virile presence seemed to overwhelmingly dominate the femininely ornamented room.

As soon as he had deposited the case and left, her mother smiled teasingly. 'Now that, as the girls in the office would way, is a spunk,' she chuckled. 'Don't you agree?'

'I guess so,' Gayna acceded, but extremely grudgingly. Personally, she was inclined to think skunk would have been more accurate!

'You guess so?' Therese half laughed, half frowned. 'I was certain he'd make more of an impression on you than that!'

He had, but not of a kind that was likely to fill Gayna with admiration! 'Well, he didn't,' she returned a little more sharply than she intended. 'Besides, I didn't come here to be impressed by any of the local males, I came to . . .'

'I know, darling, I know,' her mother broke in hurriedly, holding up a placatory hand, her sherry brown eyes filled with mute entreaty. 'But, please, don't say anything until you've given yourself time to get to know Lachlan, will you? I'm aware you think I've been horribly impulsive, but I *know* I'm doing the right thing, and before very long I'm sure you'll agree with me too.'

'Oh, Mum!' Gayna sighed helplessly. 'If I really thought you'd be happy I'd be the first to say go ahead, but . . .' she raked her fingers through her hair distractedly, 'how on earth can you possibly make such an important decision on the strength of little more than a week's acquaintance?'

'Because the feeling's right.'

'But you must have thought that . . .'

'With your father? No,' Therese shook her head sadly. 'I was only fooling myself then. I realise the difference now.'

'I still think you should give yourself more time to consider it,' Gayna argued doggedly. A chance thought had her eyeing her parent more closely, worriedly. 'You haven't set a date yet, or anything foolish like that, have you?'

'Well, apart from the fact that I don't happen to consider it foolish . . . yes, we have, as a matter of fact, though it's only a tentative one at this stage,' Therese disclosed in an annoyed-sounding tone.

'When for?' Gayna gasped. This had gone further and faster than she had even expected!

'A month's time.'

'You can't be serious!' The exclamation was out before Gayna could stop it, but on noting her mother's tightening expression, she immediately chose another tack as well as a less condemnatory voice. 'Alwyn is also—umm—worried you may be making a mistake, you know.'

'And I liked his way of expressing it even less than yours!'

Oh, hell, what had he said? Hunching one shoulder awkwardly, she offered a pacifying, 'Well, it is your interests he has at heart, after all.'

'Not entirely,' Therese contradicted drily. 'There is the little matter of the agency, remember?'

'Are you planning to sell it, then?' Gayna took the bull by the horns and asked outright.

'I haven't decided yet, but it's a distinct possibility. There are various options open to me for investment of the money which would accrue from such a sale.'

'Like, in Mundamunda?'

Initially, Therese gave a despairing shake of her head, but then, to her daughter's amazement, she started to laugh. 'You know, I could perhaps—and only *perhaps*—understand you suspecting something similar when I first phoned you, but really, Gayna, after having been flown out here in their private plane and seen this place for yourself,' waving a hand to signify their definitely not poverty-stricken surroundings, 'how can you possibly still believe the Montgomerys might be interested in *my* money? Darling, Mundamunda is huge, and I've no doubt they could buy me out half a dozen times over and still not feel the pinch.'

'Except that land, as such, isn't worth a bumper until you sell it,' Gayna could hardly wait to point out.

'Maybe not, but it still manages to provide them with an extremely profitable livelihood in the meantime, believe me! And that's besides their other business ventures,' her mother added slyly.

'Such as?'

'Cattle transports, abattoirs, other properties elsewhere ... and you've heard of Baapanannia, of course?'

Who hadn't? It might have been a mouthful, but that hadn't precluded it from being on everyone's lips recently as the newest bauxite discovery, with estimated reserves guaranteed to last for goodness knew how many years into the next century.

'So what has that to do with the Montgomerys?' she puzzled.

'They'll only be collecting royalties from every tonne that's shipped out, that's all,' Therese elucidated with obvious satisfaction at being able to deliver such a decisive *coup-de-grâce*.

Unable to quite bring herself to—or refusing to—admit that she had been wrong, Gayna grimaced sardonically, 'According to whom . . . them?'

'If, by that, you mean Lachlan and Ford, then the answer's yes. I also happen to have seen a great many genuine confirming documents too.' She gave her daughter a wry look. 'I'm not a complete incompetent when it comes to matters of business, my love, although what I do find difficult to comprehend, however, is your evident reluctance to believe they have absolutely no designs on my money.' Her head tilted quizzically to one side. 'Care to explain?'

Faced with such a direct question, Gayna could only half smile ruefully. 'I suppose because I'd already persuaded myself they did have,' she owned. Of course, a desire to find fault with Ford might also have had something to do with it since this afternoon, her thoughts ran on capriciously, but were immediately dismissed as being absurd. She didn't need any more reasons to dislike him, surely, she had enough of those already!

'But you are convinced otherwise now?' her mother persisted.

'I suppose so,' she conceded, sighing. There went one of her arguments for making her mother think twice before contemplating marriage!

CHAPTER THREE

AFTER having freshened up and changed her blouse and denim skirt for a more appropriate cotton sunfrock, Gayna accompanied her mother back to the verandah where the others had drawn their cushioned cane chairs into a semi-circle. There were three empty seats available—making her wonder if someone else wasn't also expected to join them—but rather than take the one on the end beside Ford, she seated herself beside Raeleen and left the remaining vacancy between herself and Lachlan for her mother.

'I know Therese likes an extra dry vermouth and lemonade in the afternoons, but what would you care for, Gayna?' Lachlan enquired promptly.

'The same, please,' she smiled. It was a nice light and refreshing drink.

Halfway out of his chair, he sank back into it again when his son placed his own can of beer on the table before him and rose lithely to his feet, offering, 'I'll get them,' before disappearing through the french doors behind them.

'You work in the tourist agency too, do you, Gayna?' Raeleen opened the conversation with genuine interest. 'I should imagine that dealing with travel, and all the varied places it involves, could be quite exciting at times.'

'Well, it's certainly very rarely dull, because there's so many occasions when people leave it to the last moment before deciding they want to go somewhere,' Gayna answered wryly.

'I would hardly call that *exciting*, though,' put in Felicity from Raeleen's other side on a somewhat scornful note. 'I mean, it still is only clerical work, after all, isn't it?'

'Not always,' Gayna denied with a shake of her head.

'No, in your case, I suppose not,' the blonde-haired girl laughed. 'Since it's your mother who owns the agency, I've no doubt you're the one who scores whatever free trips are in the offing.'

Unless she was very much mistaken, there had been a decided thread of malice in those words, Gayna decided, although why there should have been she had no idea. Of course Felicity had been rather aloof when they were first introduced, she went on to recall, so maybe it was just her normal manner. With an inward shrug she opened her mouth to reply and found her mother beating her to it.

'I wouldn't keep my staff very long if I played favourites like that, Felicity,' Therese smiled. 'In fact, more often than not, the reverse applies. I have to be harder on Gayna, because she's my daughter, in order to avoid any such accusations.'

Returning in time to hear her remarks, Ford handed both Therese and Gayna's drinks across simultaneously, but his eyes were locked with grey-green ones throughout.

'A disadvantage I'm sure someone with Gayna's— er—strength of character has no problem overcoming,' he bantered mockingly.

Gayna forced herself to smile along with the rest of them. They believed he was only making a joke of it, but after what he'd had to say only a short time previously about that very same character, she knew better! Accepting the tall frosty glass from him, she barely managed to nod an acknowledgment before retorting,

'But naturally! I find there's very few things I'm not able to do if I really set my mind to it.'

'That's the spirit!' applauded Lachlan, not realising she was actually referring to his relationship with her mother.

Ford was well aware of what she had meant, however, and the savage look which briefly imprinted itself on his features bore testament to the fact. Although she did notice, with a scowl, that not a trace of his annoyance was visible when he returned to his seat beside Felicity and that girl struck up a clearly fawning aside conversation with him. Oh, yes, *that* would put smiles all over his face!

'And while we're on the subject of the agency,' Therese took up where she had left off, 'once Gayna's been here for a few days, I'll have to see if her thoughts coincide with mine over my pet project of homestead holidays in the Territory. They've proved very popular on smaller properties down south, so I can't see any reason why they wouldn't be just as successful here in more remote areas.' Her next comment was directed specifically at her daughter. 'You'll have to ask Ford if he'll take you out some time when they're going after water buffalo. I went with them one day last week and enjoyed it immensely. I'm positive tourists would too,' she enthused.

Apart from the fact that she had absolutely no intention of asking Ford for anything, Gayna had other ideas on the matter. 'Couldn't that be dangerous, though?' she quizzed.

The water buffalo had originally been imported from

India more than a hundred and fifty years before but had been left to run wild after the earliest attempts to settle the north had been abandoned. Since that time they had multiplied to vast proportions, and they were large cantankerous beasts. Not the kind she would have thought it advisable to take tourists too near!

'Exactly my thoughts,' Lachlan concurred heavily.

'Oh, but they needn't actually take part,' Therese now tried another approach. 'Perhaps they could just follow in another vehicle and watch what's going on.'

'Uh-uh, still too dicey.' He evidently wasn't in favour of the idea at all. 'As you know from your own experience, it's not only the animals that are dangerous, it's the speed at which the vehicles sometimes have to travel as well. You only need to hit a stump or a termite mound, or spike a tyre, and anything could happen. The next time one of those vehicles gets rolled won't be the first, I can tell you!'

Therese looked thoughtful. 'You didn't mention any of this when you took me out,' she charged.

'I didn't want to make you nervous,' he laughed ruefully. 'But then I didn't realise you were visualising mustering water buffalo as a tourist activity either.'

'You should have,' she laughed. 'You know how doubly enthusiastic I've become about the project since I've been here.'

'Don't remind me!' he pleaded, eyes gazing skywards, then gave her a fond look. For Gayna's benefit, he explained, 'Your mother's had me flying her just about all over the Top End in her efforts to put this scheme of hers into practice. In fact,' his eyes twinkled teasingly, 'I sometimes think she only agreed to marry me in order to gain introductions to everyone I know who owns a property up here!'

'Well, how else was I likely to get them?' Therese promptly smiled in kind.

'Actually, I didn't think you'd bother with it any further, now—now that you're getting married,' Gayna interrupted stiffly.

'Oh, I couldn't just let it drop,' her mother protested. 'And especially not since I've completed so much of the spadework. Besides, I was hoping that if I didn't manage to get it all parcelled up in time, you and Alwyn might complete the arrangements for me. It would be such a shame if it failed to get off the ground for want of a few final details and some advertising.'

'Except that Alwyn and I might not be working in the agency for much longer.'

A myriad expressions flitted across her mother's face one after another, but it was amazement which lasted the longest. 'Whatever do you mean?' she exclaimed.

'Well . . .' Gayna lifted one shoulder offhandedly, 'if you sell, we could find ourselves out of work, couldn't we?'

'Wheels within wheels, eh?' was Ford's rapid gibing response, which she rewarded with a stormy gaze.

Therese came in a close second. 'That's Alwyn talking!' she accused angrily. 'What's more, it's ridiculous to even suggest such a thing! Even if I do sell, it's not likely to be for some time, and I certainly don't intend to see any of my staff lose their jobs because of it.'

'The choice may not be yours to make,' Gayna felt obliged to point out, though somewhat diffidently. She hadn't really meant to discuss this in public, but the words had just seemed to slip out—and in so doing, had given Ford just another opportunity to level the charge of selfishness against her, she realised vexedly.

'Then we'll have to make sure it is, hmm?' It was Lachlan who came to her rescue with an understanding smile. 'That is, if your mother does decide she wants to put in on the market. No one's suggested she should, you know.'

He was trying to assure her it was entirely her mother's decision, not one being forced upon her, and Gayna half smiled gratefully at him. 'No, I know,' she confessed softly. 'It was just that . . .'

'You're accustomed to thinking the worst of people,' Ford cut in again, sarcastically, bringing a smirk to Felicity's face and looks of surprise to everyone else's—except Gayna. Her expression was more like a seething glower.

'Of some, it's impossible to think badly enough!' she burst out meaningfully, acrimoniously.

'Isn't that the truth!' he was only too willing to agree.

Raeleen leant back in her chair and couldn't restrain her laughter any longer. 'Oh, I'm sorry,' she apologised, but still smiling helplessly, on finding herself the centre of everyone's attention. 'But honestly, you two sound as if you've been married for years. Are you sure you only met for the first time this afternoon?'

Gayna's face flamed with an embarrassment she tried to conceal behind her glass as she took a hopefully cooling mouthful of drink, and left it to Ford to answer his sister.

After an initial uncomplimentary snort, he did. 'You basing that considered judgment on your own personal experience, Rae?' he taunted drily.

'As if I would argue with my husband!' She looked the picture of innocence. 'Don't you remember, I promised to love and obey.'

'No, you didn't,' he had no compunction in correcting. 'You had obey replaced with keep, as I recall.'

'A vow I'm still waiting for her to begin honouring,' a cheerful voice teased from the other end of the verandah.

'Brett!' exclaimed Raeleen with a wide smile. 'When did you get back? We didn't see you come in. Would you like a drink? Come and meet Gayna.' And in an unnecessary aside to the girl next to her, 'Brett's my husband.'

Nodding, Gayna watched the jean-clad and stock-booted young man's approach, and smiled along with the others as he wryly replied to all his wife's questions.

'We rode in about thirty minutes ago, and you probably didn't see us because we returned via old Mundamunda. Yes, my oath, I'd like a drink, and,' on reaching them he held out a strong, square hand towards the youngest girl, 'the name's Brett Daniels. I'm pleased to meet you, Gayna,' he smiled.

While she was acknowledging the greeting, Ford once more disappeared inside, returning a few seconds later with three fresh cans of cold beer which he distributed among the men.

'How's that for service?' he asked humorously of his brother-in-law as they took their seats at one end of the semi-circle.

Pushing his flat-brimmed hat further back from his forehead, Brett took a long swallow before replying. 'Not bad,' he allowed with a slow bantering grin. 'But then so I reckon it should be. You've done nothing more strenuous than sit at the controls of a plane all day, and had very attractive feminine company for half of that time too, I might add.'

Gayna flushed selfconsciously and waited with indrawn breath for Ford to divulge just exactly what he had felt with regard to her presence, and then sighed in relief to hear him drawl, not too revealingly,

'Yeah, well, you just can't beat good luck, can you?' Almost immediately his voice sobered, however, as his thoughts returned to business and he questioned, 'But what made you return by way of the old homestead? It's a much longer route.'

'Mmm, don't I know it,' Brett grimaced ruefully. 'But there were signs of buffalo at the mouth of the valley, so I thought we'd better investigate.'

'And?' Lachlan sat forward to prompt.

'They're there all right,' was the heavily sighed disclosure.

'Oh, no!' Raeleen's sudden disappointed outburst seemed to mirror all their feelings, causing Gayna to frown uncomprehendingly. Seeing her expression, the dark-haired girl beside her went on to explain, 'The Valley of Lagoons is one of the prettiest places you could ever hope to see, with hot springs and everything, but if the buffalo get in there in any number they'll ruin not only the look of the place but also its grazing capabilities. Their wallowing habits can completely destroy waterholes by turning them into little more than bogs.'

Gayna nodded sympathetically, trying to picture for herself the area as Raeleen described it. 'Couldn't you fence it off, then?' she asked.

'Not from *wild* buffalo, no.' It was Lachlan who answered. 'Apart from the fact that it's impossible to erect a fence of any kind in some areas, it's just not realistic to even attempt it on such a large scale. That's

why most of the properties up here have no boundary
divisions.'

'You don't have any fences at all?'

'Only in those sections where it's absolutely necessary, and feasible,' he qualified.

'Besides, when the rains come each year and the
rivers and creeks become impassable torrents overnight, you could end up with a lot of dead cattle if
they're not free to retreat to higher ground on their
own,' added Brett.

'Then how can you keep the buffalo out of the
valley?' Gayna reverted to the original problem.

'Well, this is only the second time in . . . oh, the last
five or six years, probably, that we've found them so
far west on Mundamunda, and let's hope, if we can
clear this bunch out, it will be at least a like period
before they return,' Lachlan advised.

'Meanwhile, what do you do with them once they're
mustered . . . sell them?' she guessed.

'Too right!' Brett replied smartly. 'You can make a
tidy living just hunting and selling buffalo, what with
Europe and Asia being such big markets for their steak.
That's partly why Snow and Ford have started their
domestication programme.'

Gayna's forehead furrowed thoughtfully. 'But why
would you need to breed them when there's obviously
so many around anyway?'

'Because we'd rather replace the wild ones and keep
the species under controlled conditions instead,'
Lachlan took up the telling again. 'Since they obviously do thrive on conditions here in the Territory, as
well as being relatively easy to handle if captured young
or domestically bred, then it seemed a pity not to put
those features to some use. As they are now, however,

they're nothing but a very real threat to the pastoral industry in this country as a potential carrier of introduced diseases.'

'I see,' she nodded again, then crooked her head quizzically to one side. 'But if one of the reasons you don't want them in the Valley of Lagoons is the damage they do to waterholes, won't domesticated ones do the same thing?'

'Except that we can then control *where* they wallow to ensure they do the least amount of damage,' Ford suddenly entered the conversation, and then turned to his brother-in-law enquiringly. 'How many would you estimate there are in the valley, then?'

'Fifty, sixty or so, perhaps.'

'That many?' Lachlan's silvery grey brows lifted in surprise. 'You'd better take a trip out there tomorrow, Ford, to locate just exactly where they are, how many, and whether we'll need the chopper or not to shift them out.' And to Gayna, 'There's swamps at the head of the valley and if they're in there, a helicopter is the only thing that can get them moving.'

'Why don't we all go?' Raeleen cut in eagerly to suggest. 'It would be a good chance for Gayna to see some of the property, as well as maybe try out the thermal springs, and it's been ages since we've had a barbecue over there.'

'It's all right by me,' her father acceded in easy-going fashion. 'Ford?' looking to his son for his feelings on the matter.

Broad shoulders were flexed in a noncommittal shrug. 'I guess so,' he allowed, though to Gayna's way of thinking, not particularly enthusiastically. His blue eyes focussed on her unexpectedly. 'Can you ride?'

'Just,' she answered wryly, truthfully.

His lips curved sardonically—or was it scornfully?—but before he could comment his sister interrupted to propose, 'Gayna could come with me in the Land Rover.'

'And what about me?' asked Felicity, sounding more than a little put out.

'Well, you can take your choice,' Raeleen offered easily.

The other girl appeared far from mollified. 'But Ford promised to fly me home tomorrow!' she reminded them resentfully.

'Oh, hell!' Ford ejaculated in dismay, then followed it with a rueful grin. 'Sorry, honey, but first things first. Why don't you stay over for an extra day instead? There's no great urgency for you to return, is there?'

Evidently, since it was he who was asking, Felicity permitted herself to be persuaded. 'Not really, I suppose,' she granted with what could only have been described as a satisfied simper. 'In actual fact, I have another full week before I absolutely have to go back,' she added insinuatingly.

'Then by all means stay,' Lachlan invited generously. 'You know you're always welcome.'

'Thank you, I think I will.' Felicity could hardly keep the glow of triumph from her eyes. 'And being an extremely competent rider, myself,' modesty obviously wasn't her long suit, Gayna decided drily, 'I think I'll ride along with Ford and Brett tomorrow, and leave the Land Rover to those less able.' She eyed the man beside her with a cajoling gaze. 'Why don't we go down to the yards now so you can recommend a mount for me?'

Amiably acquiescing, Ford pushed back his chair preparing to rise, and under cover of the movement Gayna took the opportunity to clarify Felicity's gibe regarding 'those less able' by asking Raeleen in some surprise, 'Don't you ride either?'

With a laugh the older girl nodded affirmatively. 'Normally I do, but at the moment I'm pregnant, so it's not advisable.'

'Oh, I didn't realise,' Gayna smiled selfconsciously. There was certainly no thickening of Raeleen's figure to indicate her condition.

'Well, it's early days yet, so that's understandable, but . . .' Halting on seeing her brother and Felicity about to take their leave, Raeleen called out to them, 'Why don't you take Gayna with you? She might like to have a look over the place.'

With those two? Gayna could only feel a perturbing sense of dismay at the prospect. 'No, no, that's all right. I still have some things to discuss with Mum,' she evaded frantically.

'There'll be plenty of time for that later, darling. No, you go ahead and have a look round,' Therese urged fondly, and unwittingly destroying her daughter's excuse.

'Oh, but . . .'

'Perhaps Gayna isn't interested, after all,' hinted Ford, his expression goading as it rested on her becomingly flushed features, and making her fume because she suspected it was only due to her reluctance to accompany them that he was now perversely making it difficult for her to refuse to do so. He had made his feelings regarding her presence quite clear on the plane!

'I—well—naturally I am,' she stammered grudgingly. 'I just don't want to intrude, that's all.'

'On what?' The very innocence of his demeanour was a provocation in itself.

On your time with fawning Felicity, she would have liked to have retorted, but made do with an amended, 'On your time, of course.'

'In that case, since Felicity and I were only going to the yards, there's no problem, is there?' He executed a mocking half bow. 'I'm at your service.'

Swallowing the caustic, 'That'll be the day!' that rose to her lips, Gayna substituted a syrupy, 'How sweet,' and forced herself to her feet.

'That's right, lass, you get Ford to show you where everything is. He'll be only too pleased to, I'm sure,' asserted Lachlan affably as she made her way slowly across to the steps.

Weakly smiling her acknowledgment, Gayna followed the other two down to the path, and heard Felicity complaining in a mutter, 'At this rate there won't be time for any of us to do anything!'

A statement which, of course, had her steps slowing even further, until Ford, apparently guessing what she was about, dropped an arm about her shoulders in order to propel her into keeping pace with them.

'Get a move on, little sister,' he taunted. 'I may have said I was at your service, but that didn't mean for a whole week.'

'Then maybe you should have thought twice before contrarily insisting I accompany you!' she snapped. Unfortunately, the ensuing tightening of his grip had the effect of pulling her closer to his side, and from such a disquieting position she found it impossible to make her next remarks as forceful as she had intended. 'What's m—more, I—I'm not your sister, Ford Montgomery,' she denied. 'In fact, I'm not even your—your *step*sister *yet*!'

'It's only a matter of time, though,' his forecast came confidently.

'Don't count on it!' she fumed, attempting to disentangle herself from his grasp.

'Yes, well, if you've quite finished behaving so childishly, Gayna, perhaps Ford would be able to give me his arm instead of having to urge you along with it,' Felicity broke in, glaring furiously. 'I'm finding it rather difficult on this rough ground in my high heels and would certainly appreciate a helping hand.'

Even though they had left the smooth path of the garden behind, Gayna would have said the track they were now following towards the outbuildings was sandy more than anything. It definitely wasn't rough, not to her way of thinking, anyhow, but since the other girl's desire to have Ford lavish his interest solely on herself was only equalled by her own desire to be free of such attention, she was more than ready to corroborate the blonde's doubtful claims, albeit somewhat tongue-in-cheek.

'Oh dear, of course, how thoughtless of me,' she assumed the blame with mock-regret. 'It is terribly uneven, isn't it?' giving a creditable lurch herself. 'I can just imagine how you must have been suffering . . .' she paused expressively, 'in those shoes of yours.'

As soon as Felicity had voiced her grievance, Ford had considerately offered her his other arm, but to Gayna's annoyance he still hadn't removed his left one from her shoulders and she cast him a half irate, half satirical glance.

'You don't have to keep hold of me too, you know. I'm in no danger of losing *my* balance,' she gibed.

Dusky-lashed eyes surveyed her measuringly. 'No? I thought you must have been, after your stumble of a moment ago,' he returned ironically.

'A slight trip, nothing else,' she declared airily, and because he was hampered by Felicity clinging so assiduously to his right arm, she managed to free herself this time by suddenly jerking out of his reach.

After that Gayna made certain she remained a safe distance away, although as the tour progressed from shed to shed and down to the yards she did begin to wonder, ruefully, if indeed she needed to bother.

Granted, Ford had fulfilled his role as guide quite competently, if concisely, so far, but any extraneous conversation had been directed almost entirely towards Felicity—as she had originally anticipated being the case—with the result that she wasn't sure whether she ought to feel piqued or pleased by his indifference. Not that she wanted his interest, of course, but just because she refused to pander to his ego like Felicity did, there was no need for him to ignore her quite so completely, was there?

At the horse paddock, Felicity took so long deliberating over just which of the animals therein would be the most suitable for her that Gayna's attention started to wander, and it was with no little surprise that she came back to the present on hearing the other girl actually addressing her. Since that earlier sniping comment Felicity hadn't spoken to her at all.

'I'm sorry, what did you say?' she asked with a clearing shake of her head, a hasty look round explaining why the blonde had suddenly condescended to speak. Ford had temporarily disappeared.

'I enquired how long you intended staying on Mundamunda,' was the cool reply.

Gayna hunched one satin-smooth shoulder impassively. 'That depends.'

'On what?'

'My mother.' What business was it of hers, anyway?

'Oh, yes, she's done very well for herself in capturing Snow Montgomery, hasn't she? And in such short time too,' Felicity all but sneered. 'I thought it was only supposed to be the young who—er—fell in love at first sight.'

'I'm afraid Mum's always been a bit on the impetuous side,' Gayna replied as evenly as possible.

'And especially when there's money involved, hmm?'

'Meaning?' A little more sharply.

'That Snow's wealth wouldn't have had anything to do with it, of course!' Felicity's jeering was quite open now.

'No, it would not!' denied Gayna fierily. She knew her mother well enough to know that would be her last consideration in such a matter. 'Although what concern it is of yours, in any case, I've no idea!'

Felicity's lips curled disparagingly. 'Oh, don't come the innocent act with me!' she exhorted. 'Everyone's well aware that having hooked one Montgomery for herself, your mother was only too quick to see the possibilities of ensnaring the other for her, fortunately, unmarried daughter! Why else would she invite you up here at this time?'

Struggling hard to control her escalating temper, Gayna smiled tauntingly between clenched teeth. 'She didn't, Lachlan did.'

'Personally?'

'No,' warily. 'Via my mother, as a matter of fact.'

'Well, there you are, then.' The other girl shrugged meaningfully, as if her point had been proven.

'Except for one thing,' Gayna was pleased to be able to retort. '*I'm* not interested in the slightest in ensnar-

ing any male, and especially not one like Ford
Montgomery!'

'No, naturally you're not,' mocked Felicity, and
obviously totally disbelieving. 'It's just for fun that
you're trying to gain his interest by playing hard to
get!'

That was the last thing Gayna had expected to be
accused of, and involuntarily amusement suddenly
began to overtake her anger. 'It probably would be, if
I was,' she allowed in wry tones. 'However, I can
assure you I'm not. So you see, there's absolutely no
call for you to fly into a panic at the mere thought of
some competition.'

Felicity's pale cheeks flamed scarlet and her eyes
glittered menacingly. 'Don't you patronise me, you
smug little upstart!' she raged. 'And don't think I'm
going to fall for any of your lies either! I've been
watching you closely ever since you arrived and your
eyes positively burn whenever they alight on Ford!'

'More than likely,' Gayna had no hesitation in conceding, drily. 'But if you look carefully, I think you'll
find that it's with indignation . . . not infatuation.'

'Huh!' snorted Felicity in a most unfeminine
manner. 'If it was indignation, I've no doubt it would
only be due to your having failed to make any impression on him.'

Becoming bored with the whole subject, Gayna
exhaled a heavily impatient breath. 'Which fact should
make you feel very secure and happy.'

'Oh, I already do,' the older girl contended
haughtily. 'I just wanted you to realise that your pitiful
little ploy hadn't a hope of being successful, that's all.'
She gave a brittle, tinkling laugh. 'Ford prefers a more
open approach with women, thank goodness.'

'Mmm, so I noticed at the airport this afternoon,' Gayna couldn't help remarking. Felicity was really beginning to rile her. 'He had some other female, much younger than you, gushing and simpering all over him while he was there too.' It should have been her turn to smile now, but all she could raise was a disgusted grimace. 'As you say, he must like that approach, because he sure wasn't beating her off with a stick!'

Felicity looked as if she'd just been felled by one, though, as her glacial blue eyes widened in dismay and her former confidence disappeared with the speed of a deflating balloon.

Then, with a very laudable effort, she recovered sufficiently to surmise, 'Just a family friend, no doubt, or an exaggeration on your part. What was her name?'

'I wasn't interested enough to ask.'

'But you were introduced, weren't you?'

'No, I just happened to see them talking before I discovered it was Ford who was supposed to collect me,' Gayna informed her indifferently.

Having conveniently persuaded herself she had nothing to fear from the unknown girl at the airport, Felicity now pounced triumphantly. 'So you do admit you were attracted to Ford! You must have been, otherwise why would you have been watching him prior to your meeting?'

'Mainly because he represents all I dislike most in a man!' vehemently.

'Oh, yes?' Meticulously arched brows peaked sardonically. 'Who do you think you're fooling?'

'Unlike some, at least not myself!' was the pointed return.

'I wouldn't be too sure of that!'

'I don't blame you,' agreed Gayna facetiously. 'If I

were in your place, I wouldn't be too sure of anything where Ford was concerned either.'

Felicity's eyes narrowed maliciously. 'Mmm, you'd like to make me suspicious, wouldn't you? You think that would make it easier for you and your mother to continue with your nefarious little scheme. Well, it won't work!' she announced spiritedly. 'I'm wide awake to what you're up to, no matter what far-fetched denials you think you can fob me off with!'

'Then I guess there's nothing more to be said,' Gayna shrugged. It was of little interest to her whether the other girl believed her or not, provided she let the matter drop. She scanned the yards and outbuildings cursorily. 'Where is Ford, anyway?'

'Why do you want to know?'

'Oh, for heaven's sake!' Gayna exploded incredulously. Wasn't she even permitted to mention the man's name? 'Because if he doesn't return shortly, I'm going back to the homestead, that's why!' She'd seen most of what there was to see, and she didn't intend standing around bandying pleasantries with Felicity until he deigned to return.

'He's gone to make arrangements for tomorrow,' Felicity then consented to divulge, but added slyly, 'He could still be a while yet, though.'

'Well, whether he is or not, I think I'll be off in any case,' Gayna decided unconcernedly, moving away from the rail she had been leaning against. 'I'll see you at dinner.'

'What shall I tell him, *if* he should bother to ask why you didn't wait?' Felicity called jeeringly after her.

'Try the truth . . . that I found your limited conversation boring beyond belief!' Gayna recommended just as derisively over one shoulder, and continued on her way.

No sooner had she rounded the corner of the first outbuilding, however, than she promptly collided with someone coming from the opposite direction and two hard hands held her arms fast to steady her.

'Where are you off to in such a hurry?' queried Ford wryly.

Pulling free without too much trouble on this occasion, Gayna tilted her head in a somewhat defiant gesture. 'Back to the house. Any objections?'

'Where you're concerned, quite a few,' he responded bluntly. 'Where's Felicity?'

'Waiting patiently where you left her.'

'Patience not being a virtue of yours, I gather?'

'Where you're concerned, no,' she copied pertly. 'Now, if you'll excuse me . . .' She made to step past him.

'I don't!' A muscular arm looped about her midriff to force her back against the wall of the building and kept her pinned there as mocking blue eyes connected with wide and startled green. 'So now what are you going to do about it, hmm?'

'Kick your damned shins to pieces, if you're not careful!' she threatened wrathfully.

He spared a glance at her open-toed footwear and his mouth curved ironically upwards. 'I doubt that would be possible in those, but I wouldn't advise it, anyhow. That is, not if you intend sitting at all during the next few days.'

'Big, tough man, huh?' she gibed insolently.

'Well, somebody sure needs to be while there's a spoiled, argumentative brat like you around!' he retaliated in an arrogant voice. 'It's a pity your mother

didn't remarry years ago, if only to provide you with
the firm handling you so obviously require!'

'I'm beginning to think it's a pity she didn't too! At
least then I wouldn't have had to suffer meeting you!'
she hurled back at him. 'And as for your *firm handling*,'
with seething emphasis, 'well, I suggest you reserve
your ideas on that for your horses, because no man
ever has, or ever will, control me!'

'Aren't you forgetting something?' Ford drawled,
eyeing significantly the arm which was, in truth, keeping her in check at that very moment.

'Oh, very witty!' she commanded acidly. 'You must
really slay 'em in the aisles at the local cattlemen's
meeting.' Her eyes widened tauntingly. 'So what do
you do for an encore?'

'I know what I feel like doing!'

'Something original, I hope,' she mocked. 'I find
your chauvinistic ideas of physical retribution too tedi-
ous for words.'

'Then let's see if this can't enliven proceedings for
you!'

Before she could even guess at his meaning, Gayna
abruptly found her chin captured by an inescapable
hand and her soft mouth crushed beneath his in a hard
and forceful kiss which not only took her breath away
with its unexpectedness, but temporarily had her
emotions floundering out of control.

Caught firmly against his rugged form, she was
being made all too aware of him in a strictly physical
sense, as well as suddenly realising her lips were way-
wardly beginning to part, and in a panic she strove to
break the wholly perturbing contact. Perhaps because
his action had been so completely unanticipated, but it
was the first time ever that her head hadn't been fully

in charge of her responses in such a situation, and she castigated herself angrily for letting this man, of all people, be the first to get under her guard, even momentarily.

'You—you . . . don't you dare do that again!' she half blazed, half spluttered when at last she was free to speak again. Not through her efforts, but because he had finally consented to release her. 'No man kisses me unless *I* say so!'

Gazing down into her furious features, Ford grinned impenitently. 'That being the case, you really did get what you wanted, didn't you?'

'Meaning?'

'Something original,' he reminded her drily.

She wiped the back of her hand insultingly across her mouth. 'I didn't also ask for something so unpalatable, though, did I?'

A slow lazy smile edged its way across his shapely moulded mouth, exasperatingly holding her mesmerised. 'I wasn't aware that it was. At least, not until you realised how willingly you were responding,' he taunted. 'I was rather more of the opinion it was your own reaction you found unpalatable.'

'Don't flatter yourself!' she retorted defensively, embarrassedly. Unfortunately, he wasn't entirely wrong. 'I've been kissed by better men than you and remained unmoved!'

'Mmm.' He chucked her aggravatingly under the chin. 'But apparently only on your terms. It's a pity they didn't take the initiative, then they might also have discovered how fragile that veneer of imperviousness which you flaunt so proudly really is.'

'That's no veneer, it's a solid wall!' she averred defiantly.

'You think so?' he goaded, laughing. 'It might have been once, sweetheart, but a moment ago it had cracks in it a mile wide, I can assure you.'

'Well, that at least relieves my mind, because any assurances I receive from men of your kind I automatically disbelieve!' she relayed disdainfully.

'In other words, you'd rather delude yourself than face the truth! From what Therese has had to say, you must take after your father in that regard.'

No one had ever likened Gayna to her irresponsible father before—in any regard—and, as a consequence, Ford's sudden accusation stunned her into miserable silence. Then, with a betraying tremble to her lips, she caught him unprepared and thrust herself away from him.

'That's a lie!' she repudiated vehemently. 'I'm nothing at all like him . . . *nothing at all*! Do you hear?' And spinning about she began running for the homestead.

'*Gayna!*'

Behind her, Ford's voice sounded in a mixture of surprise and impatience, but she neither turned nor stopped. All she wanted was to reach the safety of her room unseen in order to recover her composure in private. Not all of which, she realised in some agitation, had been caused by his last distressing accusation.

CHAPTER FOUR

It wasn't until breakfast the following morning that Gayna discovered her mother and Lachlan had decided against accompanying the rest of them to the valley that day, and as Therese and herself left the dining room together she set about trying to change her mother's mind.

'But I naturally expected you and Lachlan to be coming with us,' she told her. 'You haven't already seen the valley, have you?'

'No, but there'll be plenty of other occasions for me to see it, I'm sure,' Therese reasoned plausibly.

'Why not now, while I'm here?' persuasively.

Therese sighed regretfully. 'Well, for one thing, I want to give Alwyn another call today, and as well as that, Lachlan is expecting some important business calls of his own.'

'Then why didn't you say so when the idea was first mentioned?'

'Because it just didn't occur to me you might think we *were* going.'

'But Raeleen said "all" of us.'

'I know she did, darling, but she was really only meaning you younger ones. I thought you must have known that. Besides,' Therese half laughed, 'I can't see why it should make you quite so disturbed whether we go or not. You don't need a pair of chaperones, do you?' She slanted her daughter an extremely wry glance. 'Or are you just upset because it prevents you from chaperoning me?'

'No, of course not!' Gayna protested earnestly. In truth, that hadn't entered her mind. However, she did pause to wonder if her mother's teasing remark about requiring a chaperone herself might have been closer to the mark than either she wanted, or Therese realised. She really wasn't looking forward to spending the day in Ford's disturbing company, even though the other three would also be present. The events of the previous afternoon were still too fresh in her thoughts for her to be able to treat him with as much equanimity as she would have liked. 'I—it's just that— considering Raeleen said the place was so pretty—I thought it would be nice for us to see it together, that's all,' she concluded lamely.

'Yes, well, if Lachlan and I weren't so busy, I'm sure it would have been,' her mother smiled soothingly. 'Never mind, though, at least it should be an interest-ing start to your holiday.'

'I didn't come here for a holiday,' Gayna reminded her flatly.

'I'm well aware of that,' Therese's tone sharpened markedly. 'But that doesn't mean you can't—at least, for my sake—pretend to enjoy yourself while you're here, does it? I mean, you haven't exactly put yourself out to be friendly since you arrived, and at dinner last night not only did you hardly speak to Felicity, but you were positively glaring daggers at poor Ford throughout the whole meal. Goodness only knows what they've done to deserve such treatment!'

With a caustic grimace Gayna proceeded to en-lighten her, skimpily. 'I'm sorry, but Felicity's type of haughty behaviour just doesn't appeal to me, so I figure it's best if I don't have much to say to her,' she disposed of that girl perfunctorily. 'As for Ford,' drawing in a deep calming breath, 'well, let's just say we didn't hit it off from the time we met. He's arrogant, self-centred . . . and he had the absolute gall to imply that I was as superficial as my father!' she burst out resentfully, and quite unintentionally. But having done so, she then thumped her hands on to her hips and went on to charge bitterly, 'What in hell would he know!'

'Gayna!' Therese remonstrated lightly with a frown at her daughter's language, but didn't press the matter. 'I can perhaps understand your feelings with regard to Felicity—I must admit I don't find her personality particularly inviting either—although, since she's a friend of Raeleen's, I do think you could make little more of an effort to disguise your attitude.'

'And Ford?' Gayna cued in sardonic accents.

Her mother's lips pursed and then twitched somewhat humorously. 'What *can* I say after that outburst?' she countered. 'You already know I think he's a real charmer . . .'

'Oh, he's that all right!'

'. . . but with regard to him saying you're like your father . . .' Therese continued, ignoring the scornful interruption.

'Superficial, like my father!' Gayna cut in once more to qualify.

'Oh, darling, did he really say that?' Her mother sighed, shaking her head helplessly.

'Maybe not in so many words, but that was what he meant!'

'But why? What had you done to make him say such a thing?'

Recalling just what she had said, and why, Gayna
immediately put it out of her mind again. There were
some things she wasn't prepared to discuss, even with
her mother!

'Er—I don't remember,' she parried instead. 'But
whatever it was, he's wrong!' Her gaze, as it rested on
her mother, became a little less confident. 'Isn't he?'

'By thinking your nature is as shallow as your
father's was? Yes, of course he is, love,' her mother
reassured her promptly, adamantly. 'Although I'm
afraid, whether you dislike the idea or not, there are
ways in which you do resemble him.'

'You've never said so before!' Gayna accused,
aghast.

'I've never really had a reason to raise the matter
before, and especially in view of your having always
been so critical of your father,' Therese explained excusingly.

'So were you!'

'Not quite to the same extent, though. I was at least
prepared to concede that none of us is perfect, and to
eventually forgive Everett his weaknesses.' She smiled
a little sadly. 'Considering the outcome, I guess I
haven't really been above reproach myself, have I?'

'In what way?'

'In condemning Everett so openly in your presence
when you were at such a young and impressionable
age, and then compounding the error by allowing you
to continue thinking so censoriously of him when you
were older.'

'I doubt you could have stopped me,' Gayna half
laughed, half grimaced. 'As soon as I was older, I could
see the truth for myself. Men aren't to be trusted!'

'That's just the point I'm making,' Therese tried to

impress on her. 'Men aren't all the same, as you appear to have convinced yourself!'

'No?' Gayna eyed her cynically, and then shrugged and granted in facetious tones, 'No, I guess you're right. Some *are* decidedly worse than others . . . and the smooth-talking, self-centred, good-looking ones are the worst of the lot!'

'Oh, Gayna!' Her mother bit at her lip sorrowfully. 'How could I have been so foolish as to think you would grow out of those early childhood sentiments? I thought once you were old enough to have a boy-friend or two you would soon realise how misguided you'd been, but for some unknown reason the opposite seems to have taken place. The more men you come to know, the less you seem to think of them!'

'Maybe I just attract the undesirable type,' Gayna quipped.

'But you couldn't possibly have said that nice . . .'

'Let's not rake over old ground, Mum,' Gayna broke in adamantly, holding up a quelling hand. 'As you've just informed me that I do take after my father, I reckon I've got enough problems without resurrecting old ones.'

'You should be grateful you take after him in some respects,' chided Therese gently. She reached out to tap Gayna softly on the cheek. 'Where else do you think you got that beautiful bone structure from, hmm?'

'But I resemble you!' Gayna fought against such an association, eyeing her mother's rich auburn hair and instinctively raising a hand to her own copper locks.

'Only in colouring. I may have what are generally regarded as regular features, but I know my limitations, darling, and a raving beauty I'm not! No, those

looks of yours, which you always discount so readily,
are a legacy from your father, not from me.' Therese
would accept none of the credit.

Never having seen a decent photograph of her other
parent—in a moment of bitter resentment Therese had
thrown out all bar a few hazy snapshots when Everett
had first deserted them—Gayna was in no position to
dispute her mother's astonishing claims and, as a
result, she was left her with very little to say.

'Yes, well, that's enough of a revelation for one day,
I think. Let's talk about something else, shall we?'
Then, remembering Ford's assertions of the day
before, her mouth crooked sardonically. 'Or would that
be construed as deluding myself and refusing to face
the truth?'

Therese hunched one shoulder indecisively, but
before she could offer any comment, one way or the
other, Raeleen appeared in the doorway leading on to
the front verandah.

'You nearly ready, Gayna?' she called. 'The Land
Rover's just about packed.'

'I'll be right with you,' went back the answering
shout. And to her mother, 'You're sure you can't
come?'

'Not this time, love, I'm sorry.'

'So be it, I guess,' Gayna ruefully accepted the inevitable with a sigh. 'I'll see you when we return,
then.'

'Mmm, but in the meantime . . .' Therese sent her a
persuasive smile, 'do try and enjoy yourself, won't you,
Gayna, and—and not be too quick to judge?' she suggested hopefully.

Unable to give a blanket assurance—there were
others involved, after all—Gayna came as close as she

could. 'I can't promise anything, but I will give it a try,' she vowed wryly.

Surmising that that was probably as good as she could expect, Therese accompanied her daughter to her room in order to collect the carryall Gayna had already packed in readiness and then out to the front of the homestead to wave farewell.

The back of the vehicle was filled with a variety of equipment, Gayna noticed on taking her seat beside Raeleen. There were ropes and pieces of riding tack; spare tyres and a box of replacement motor parts. A machete, an axe, and a couple of rifles; a jerrycan of fuel; two bulging saddlebags and a pair of carryalls similar to her own—which she presumed belonged to Raeleen and Felicity. Three large plastic containers of drinking water and a first aid kit; a couple of portable fridges, and last but not least, two bright-eyed cattle dogs which were obediently curled up behind the front seats.

'We're ready for any emergency, I see,' laughed Gayna, and nodded over her shoulder to indicate the load behind them as soon as they were under way.

'You have to be up here when you never know what's likely to happen once you head into the bush,' her companion smiled in return.

'And the dogs? Do you always take them too?'

'If possible. They save you a tremendous amount of time and effort when you're working cattle, besides being invaluable in other ways.'

'Such as?'

'On picnics,' Raeleen supplied with a chuckle. 'Nothing spoils the atmosphere more than for a damned great snake to come slithering out of the undergrowth, but they,' gesturing towards the dogs, 'can smell them out long before you ever set eyes on them.'

Turning, Gayna patted each of the animals in turn. 'Good dogs,' she praised drily.

As they passed the horse yards without stopping, Raeleen explained, 'The others left about fifteen minutes ago. They're planning to cut across that ridge over there,' pointing to her right. 'It's quicker than following the road. We'll probably catch up to them just as they're reaching the valley.'

Gayna nodded, her forehead already beginning to crease with a recurring thought. 'If the valley's so pretty, though, why was the location of the homestead changed?'

'Because when the family first moved in here late last century they didn't realise—no one did,' Raeleen half laughed ruefully, 'just how much rain does fall in the wet, or how all the rivers, creeks and lagoons can overflow to form enormous inland lakes covering hundreds of square miles. The result was that the old homestead invariably had water lapping at its walls, if not inside, every summer. So when my grandfather decided the place needed additional rooms—he had thirteen children—rather than enlarge the old homestead he re-sited it altogether and built a new one where the floods couldn't reach it.'

'Which accounts for it being so large, I suppose. To accommodate all those children,' commented Gayna wryly.

'Yes, well, big families were the norm in the outback in those days. They still are in a lot of instances. With such large properties to run it's handy to have a number of children ... especially if there's a preponderance of boys,' Raeleen added with a chuckle.

After that their conversation was mostly desultory as Raeleen pointed out various things of note and Gayna took in the tropical scenery with interest. At least her mother was right in one respect, she mused contemplatively. The area did have tremendous potential for viewing wildlife in its natural state. In that regard it was an, as yet, untapped paradise, for there were birds of every description—red-tailed black cockatoos, impressive Jabiru storks, and honking magpie geese; blue-faced honey-eaters, ibis, and red-collared lorikeets.

On the ground there were just as many attractions to catch her interest too. Magnetic termite mounds—wrongly called 'anthills' at times—some reaching unbelievable heights, but always facing north to south so that one side was always in the shade in order to keep their eggs cool; kangaroos, wallabies and emus; while on the sandy edge of a billabong they passed two thin-snouted crocodiles basking in the warm morning sunlight.

'There's none of those where we're going, I hope,' Gayna remarked ruefully, trying to repress an involuntary shudder at the sight of the primeval reptiles.

'No, although the freshwater crocodiles, which those two are, are harmless enough,' Raeleen sympathetically put her mind at rest. 'Not like the salties, or estuarine crocodiles, you find round the coast, I'm glad to say. They're much larger than these, and since there's been a ban on shooting them for the last ten years or so, they've become almost fearless of man and are now beginning to cause some considerable concern by the way their numbers are multiplying and spreading into every conceivable waterway in the north, because they'll attack, and without provocation.'

'Lovely creatures!' This time Gayna did give a shiver. 'You're positive these aren't the same species?'

'I'm positive!' her companion confirmed decisively. 'You wouldn't catch me round any of these waterholes if they weren't! Anyway, they're easy enough to tell apart. The freshwater ones, besides being considerably smaller, have very pointed snouts, whereas the salties have a blunt and much broader head.'

'I'll keep it in mind,' vowed Gayna before returning her attention to her surroundings.

They were heading into more thickly wooded country now where bloodwoods and stringybark vied with towering stands of bamboo, pandanus, and cycad palms, and where the lagoons were covered with beautiful pink lotus lilies, or the equally attractive blue, mauve and white waterlilies. Around the thickly grassed edges of these pools were also the first grazing cattle Gayna had seen, their great humped backs denoting their Brahman breed, their hides sleek and well filled. To their left a couple of brumbies—wild horses—suddenly made their appearance, startling the cattle for a moment before they resumed their contented feeding, and then taking fright themselves on hearing the Land Rover and disappearing back into the undergrowth as quickly and nervously as they had burst from it.

Just as abruptly, the track they were following made a sharp turn of its own in order to seek a path around— or so Gayna thought—a series of tree-shrouded cliffs they had been steadily approaching. Instead, she saw to her surprise, it began to climb a small spur which led directly between the cliffs, then sloped gently on the other side to the floor of a lush green valley.

'The Valley of Lagoons,' announced Raeleen, bringing the vehicle to a halt at the top of the rise. 'What do you think of it?'

'Beautiful, just beautiful,' Gayna sighed appreciatively. Protected along two sides by far-reaching arms of sandstone, fertile pastures interspersed with areas of tropical growth and dotted with shining lagoons stretched for miles towards a blue-hazed horizon. 'No wonder you don't want buffalo ruining it.'

'Mmm, it would be a shame, wouldn't it?' As she smiled across at her passenger, Raeleen's brows peaked questioningly. 'Feel like walking around for a bit? It seems as if we've beaten the others, after all, so we may as well wait for them here.'

'Suits me,' Gayna shrugged negligently, opening her door. If she had to contend with Ford and Felicity for a day, she supposed this was as good a place as any to start. At least the scenery was soothing, even if they weren't!

Nevertheless, no sooner had they alighted from the vehicle than they heard the sound of horses behind them, and Gayna could feel herself tensing warily as the other three crested the hill a couple of minutes later.

'I'm surprised we didn't see you on the other side of the hill. You could only have been a minute or so behind us,' Raeleen smiled cheerfully.

'We were,' Brett acknowledged. 'We saw you and gave a shout, but I guess we must have been too far back among the trees for you to see or hear.'

'It's been a glorious ride, though,' put in Felicity on a contented sigh, resting her hands on the pommel of her saddle. 'You should try it some time, Gayna, it's quite an experience.' With an exaggerated gasp and a slightly smug glance she corrected herself. 'Oh, I forgot, you don't ride very well, do you?'

'No, not particularly,' Gayna didn't mind admitting. 'But then I'm a real city girl at heart, and I'd rather drive than ride, in any case.'

'You mean you prefer living in the city?' The other girl sounded incredulous.

Gayna's lips twisted wryly. 'That's right. There's a lot of us who have never experienced the slightest desire to live anywhere else but in the city, you know. I'm not the only one.'

Felicity appeared to take that as almost a personal affront. 'Then why come with us today if you dislike the bush so much?' she demanded.

'I didn't say I disliked the bush,' Gayna contradicted patiently. 'In fact, I've found the trip extremely interesting so far. I merely said I had no wish to live out here.'

Ford, who until now had remained silent on Felicity's far side, suddenly tightened his reins and heeled his mount into movement. 'Right, now if you two have quite finished your little dissertation, perhaps we can continue on into the valley, hmm?' he suggested with no little sarcasm.

'Yes, of course.' Felicity very smartly had her palomino edging up beside him.

Gayna returned to her transport less rapidly, her eyes grey and moody as they surveyed the three riders heading down the track. Now what had caused that piece of satiric brusqueness? she wondered. Surely he couldn't have taken exception to anything she'd said . . . or was he also of the opinion that just because he preferred living in the outback, then everyone else should as well? With a dismissive shake of her head she took her seat in the Land Rover and determinedly put the matter out of her mind. Why should she bother herself with what he thought, anyway? Right from the beginning it had been perfectly obvious their views weren't likely to coincide on any subject!

The old homestead was situated about a third of the way down the valley, and when they pulled up beside the mellowed sandstone ruins Gayna could well understand how those first Montgomerys could have been deceived into selecting such a site. At the side of the house the palm-fringed thermal pool with its crystal clear water and sandy bottom was a delight to behold, while the string of lily-clad lagoons which formed a pink and blue chain at the rear of the building looked so tranquil against their emerald backdrop of tropical vegetation that it was almost impossible to imagine them ever becoming a danger.

The unloading of the picnic gear from the Land Rover was the first task undertaken, but immediately it had been completed Felicity extracted her bag from the vehicle and began moving towards the house.

'I'm going to have a swim,' she announced, expressively lifting the heavy coil of blonde hair from her neck. 'How about you, Rae?'

'Sounds great,' her friend answered no less enthusiastically, then sent her husband and brother a perceptive encompassing glance. 'I guess you two will be wanting to check on the buffalo, though, won't you?'

'That's the reason we came,' Ford drawled as he prepared to swing back into the saddle.

Brett, on the other hand, hesitated a moment before remounting, his hazel eyes settling on Gayna. 'Why don't you come with us?' he proposed in friendly tones. 'Prince is quiet enough for a beginner,' indicating the palomino, 'and it's easy riding for most of the way.'

So totally unprepared was she for the suggestion that

momentarily Gayna could only stare at him in surprise, and then found her gaze annoyingly travelling on to Ford as if to gauge his reaction to the proposal. A gaze which encountered such a mocking expression in return that she promptly, selfconsciously, redirected it towards Brett.

In the meantime, Felicity had come to an abrupt halt and was now hastily retracing her steps. 'Oh, well, if I'd known you were . . .' she began.

'No, you go ahead and have your swim. You kept saying how much you were looking forward to it,' Brett cut her off with unexpected peremptoriness. He turned to the younger girl again to prompt, 'Well, what about it, Gayna?'

'I—er . . .' She shook her head regretfully. 'It's very nice of you to suggest it, but I . . .'

'Not game, huh?'

There was only one person who would interrupt with such a gibing remark and she spun to face him resentfully. 'That has nothing to do with it!' she flared. Why he, out of all of them, should be attempting to goad her into going she had no idea. Unless, of course, he was enjoyably anticipating her making a fool of herself! 'And if Felicity would rather go . . .' She allowed her words to trail away explicitly.

'No, Felicity would rather swim.' Strangely, or perhaps not so strangely in view of her previous supposition, it was Ford who vetoed the blonde accompanying them this time, Leaning sideways, he untethered the palomino and proffered the reins to her. 'So if it's not nerves that's stopping you . . .' He proved he was also capable of leaving things significantly unsaid.

He made it sound as if she was nervous of *him*! Gayna smouldered indignantly, and in her desire to show him how mistaken he was almost snatched the reins from his outstretched hand.

'Well, don't say I didn't warn you if I make a mess of things, will you?' she grimaced tauntingly as she swung on to the gelding's back.

'As if we would!' It was Brett who replied, unaware that she had intended the retort for the man beside him.

'Oh, you'll need a hat!' exclaimed Raeleen just as they were about to leave, and hurrying across to the Land Rover, retrieved her friend's. 'Here, Felicity won't be needing hers.'

'But I . . .' Felicity immediately started to remonstrate.

'Surely you don't mind?' Raeleen slanted her a deeply surprised look.

Felicity at least had the grace to blush. 'Er—no, I suppose not,' she smiled weakly, grudgingly, realising her friend had really made it impossible for her to refuse. Even so, she still just had to add, 'But she'd better look after it, because it's almost brand new, and I don't want it ruined!'

'Oh, I'm sure she will, won't you, Gayna?' Raeleen smiled as she handed the wide-brimmed covering up to her.

Settling it securely on her coppery tresses, Gayna returned the smile wryly. 'If necessary, as if my life depended upon it,' she averred ironically. Anything less would probably be considered purposely remiss by Felicity!

'How long do you expect to be gone?' Raeleen now asked her husband.

'The rest of the morning, probably.'

'That long?' burst out Felicity in a complaining

voice. 'I thought you said on the way out here that you'd be away for hardly any time at all.'

Brett hunched solid shoulders impassively. 'When you're used to spending whole days in the saddle, a few hours *is* hardly any time at all,' he drawled.

Giving him a glare of arctic intensity and stifling something which sounded remarkably like the grinding of teeth, Felicity turned on her heel and went storming back towards the house, leaving her friend to chide drily,

'You, my love, can be an infuriating heel on occasion.'

'Mmm, I know,' he agreed without a hint of remorse, and urging his mount forward, bent to drop a light kiss on her upturned forehead. 'But then I've never been able to take more than a little of Felicity at one time.'

What Raeleen had to say to that Gayna didn't hear. She was too occupied in absorbing the realisation that Brett wasn't overly enamoured of his wife's friend either! And no sooner had that information been assimilated than she flashed a covert glance from beneath the cover of her long lashes to see what effect the revelation had on Ford. But as soon as she noted the completely unperturbed set of his good-looking features, her lips began to curve scornfully. No, of course it wouldn't worry him what his brother-in-law thought of Felicity, because no matter what that girl might like to persuade herself into believing, he wasn't interested in her in any amorous fashion. His only interest in her was as a bolster for his ego—just like the girl at the airport! The self-opiniated louse!

Hard on the heels of this thought, however, came another. That Brett might only have suggested she accompany them in an effort to make certain Felicity didn't and the idea had her swiftly reverting her gaze to Raeleen's husband.

'Now that Felicity's—umm—definitely decided to go for a swim, perhaps you would rather just go with Ford, after all,' she offered deprecatingly.

Brett saw through her reasoning immediately. 'Uh-uh, don't be a goose,' he admonished amiably. 'I just thought you might like your initial view of the buffalo to be while they're in their natural state, instead of when they're being mustered, and galloping all over the place.'

'I see. Well, yes, as a matter of fact, I would,' she smiled with shy gratitude.

'Then let's go.' He unthinkingly slapped his hand down on to the gelding's rump, startling Prince into action and causing Gayna to wonder if she was going to be unseated even before they'd started until she managed to eventually regain control. 'We'll see you at lunch,' he called to Raeleen as they broke into a steady canter with one of the dogs following, while the other obediently, but dejectedly, remained behind as commanded.

It was some time since Gayna had last been riding and, coupled with today's inauspicious beginning, it took her a while to relax, but as the track proved to be as easy as Brett had predicted, and Prince a smooth-gaited animal, she at last felt some of her nervous tension leaving her.

Halfway down the valley they slowed to a walk, the men spreading out into the belly-high grass on either side of the narrow track, their practised eyes already seeing signs which went unnoticed by Gayna. Ford was the first to actually come across any of the buffalo and, signalling for silence, he beckoned her over to him.

'There, up ahead.' He gestured to a waterhole some hundred yards in front of them as she reached his side.

For a moment Gayna couldn't distinguish the animals from their surroundings, but then a movement alerted her to their exact whereabouts and enabled her to make out the heavily horned, grey-coated beasts as they lay half submerged in mud at the edge of the waterhole.

'Did they turn the edges of that pool into such a quagmire?' she frowned. It was certainly an unprepossessing sight after all the beautiful lagoons they'd passed.

'Mmm, and if they're left there, it will just deteriorate further and further.'

'Which would be a tragedy,' she sighed. That waterhole must have been as pretty as the others before the buffalo arrived. Easing Prince's head round, she prepared to return to the track. 'Well, thank you for showing them to me, anyway.'

'Hold it!' Ford's hand caught at her reins before she could complete her move. 'You'd better stay with me from now on. It'll be safer.'

'For whom?' The caustic quip slipped out before she could forestall it.

A lazy smile slowly etched its way over his attractively moulded lips and, unaccountably, had Gayna's pulse racing at the sight of it. 'Believe it or not, for you, sweetheart,' he mocked. 'As I hadn't expected you to be coming with us, I didn't bother to bring one of the rifles along.'

'Why should my presence make any difference? Or is it me you'd like to shoot?' She sent him a facetious gaze filled with sarcasm.

'Don't put ideas into my head!' His recommendation was drily made. Then he returned to a more serious mien. 'The difference is, you obviously haven't enough riding experience—and especially in this type of country—to get yourself out of any trouble that could occur with these animals.'

'Such as?'

'They have a nasty habit of charging if you annoy them.'

Not a particularly cheering prospect, she had to admit. 'That didn't seem to worry you when you all but goaded me into coming,' she recalled with a grimace.

'Probably because I'm not planning to annoy them, just count 'em,' he drawled as he began moving once more.

'Well, good for you! But what about me?' she demanded of his broad back as she followed.

'I wouldn't advise you to upset them either.'

Gayna's mouth pulled into a disgruntled line. 'And just how, might I ask, do I avoid doing that?'

'By staying close and doing as you're told,' he counselled with a taunting grin. 'That, in itself, will probably be a novelty for you.'

'Where you're concerned it will be unique, I can promise you that!' she wasn't above retaliating with some tartness. Even under these circumstances, the idea of taking orders from him didn't come easy.

'Then I suggest you start by keeping quiet,' he voiced his first command wryly. 'And you'd better come round here,' indicating the near-side of his mount. 'To keep you out of the line of fire, as it were. I'm sure Therese would never forgive me if anything happened to her spoiled little darling.'

Obeying his instructions, she flashed him a simmering green glare. 'Your gallantry almost overwhelms me!' she gibed. 'But hadn't you better keep quiet too? Or doesn't *your* talking disturb the buffalo?' with honeyed emphasis.

Apparently he must have thought it possible because, after contenting himself with an extremely expressive glance in response, he didn't speak again until they had carefully made their way past that particular group of animals and were out in the clear once more.

'Well, what do you think of Therese and Snow getting married now that you've had a chance to see them together?' he then caught her off guard by asking.

Her ensuing shrug was almost defiant. 'I'm still against it!'

'But surely even you, preconceived ideas notwithstanding, must be able to see how happy they are together!' he charged in a low, rigidly controlled tone.

'It's not *now* that concerns me!' she retorted on a flaring note. 'It's six months or six years hence that I'm worried about! How happy are they going to be then?'

'There's only one way to find out . . . wait and see!' Metallic blue eyes flicked over her derisively. 'Or are you suggesting that's the length of time they should wait before making a decision?'

'At least that would make more sense than rushing into it like they are doing! And if it comes to that,' her eyes narrowed suspiciously, 'what's in it for you, anyway, that you're so anxious to see them married?'

A muscle corded tightly in his jaw and his mouth set into a hard line. 'There's nothing *in it* for me, as you so charmingly put it,' his denial was ground out scathingly, 'except that I happen to be able to recognise two lonely people who are not only right for each other, but who also have a genuine regard for one another!'

'After only two weeks?' she scoffed, her chin angling higher to challenge his unconcealed scorn.

'Sometimes one *day* is enough!'

'Oh, yeah, sure! That's what Mum thought with my father, and look where it got her!'

'Where it got her ... or you?' he countered, contempt predominant.

Gayna's breasts rose and fell sharply as a result of her deepened breathing. 'And just what's that supposed to imply?'

'That you're the only one who appears to have any hang-ups regarding your father, and the length of time he stayed married to Therese! So much so, in fact, that one gets the impression it's your feelings you're mostly concerned about, not your mother's!'

'That's not true!' she heaved irately. 'You're just trying to find fault with me because I won't agree with you! Although while we're on the subject, what makes you so competent to judge whether my mother's lonely or not, anyhow?'

'Maybe because I bother to pay some attention to her feelings. You should try it some time, instead of always considering yourself first!' he flayed witheringly.

'So you keep saying ... *ad nauseam*!' she blazed. How dared he insinuate that she never paid any attention to her mother's feelings! It was to protect just those feelings that she had come to Mundamunda. 'And if you think I'm going to sit here listening to you repeat yourself all morning, then you've got another think coming, because I'm going back to the homestead!'

'Oh, no, you're not! You're staying right here,' he vetoed arbitrarily, reaching out for the gelding's bridle as Gayna began turning away.

'That's what you think!' She slapped at his hand furiously, and abruptly found her wrist imprisoned instead of her mount's headgear.

Too incensed to admit she might have been fighting a losing battle, she immediately dropped the reins altogether in order to renew the attack with her other hand, but only succeeded in dealing him one ineffectual blow to the arm before Prince took the first of a few shuffling forward steps.

Taking into account the angle at which she was already leaning, as well as the inexorably widening gap between the two animals, the outcome was a foregone conclusion, and with a quickly indrawn gasp of dismay Gayna started to slide ignominiously downwards, to land with a decided thump on her seat in the dirt.

From her newly low position she glared upwards into an unabashedly amused face. 'Oh, yes, you let go then, didn't you?' she accused hotly.

'If I hadn't, you probably would have broken your arm, or at least dislocated a shoulder,' he drawled. 'As it is, all that's hurt is your dignity.'

Gayna wasn't so sure. One part of her anatomy was distinctly tender, she found ruefully, on scrambling to her feet and brushing herself down. Nor was she in any mood to accept even the most logical of excuses.

'You still could have made some effort to help,' she complained resentfully as she began looking about for her hat which had been displaced during her fall. 'Or was that too much to expect?'

There was no time for Ford to reply, because at that moment she located her hat, being well and truly trampled beneath Prince's hind legs, and she rushed forward to retrieve it with a despairing wail.

'Oh, now look at it! It's ruined! Felicity will never forgive me ... and she'll probably think I did it on purpose,' she surmised glumly, trying to push the battered felt back into some semblance of its original shape.

'Mmm, I doubt she'll be too pleased.' And the fact that he laughed as he said it in no way served to pacify her ruffled feelings.

Clapping the now rather floppy-brimmed hat back on her head, she remounted with a stormy look on her face. 'Of course, you realise it's all your fault! If you'd let me return to the homestead, as I wanted, Felicity's hat would still be as good as new.'

'And if you'd done as you were told, for once in your life, it still would be too,' he retorted in an acidly humorous voice. 'Now let's get a move on, or Brett will be wondering what's happened to us.'

With her attempted defiance having brought about nothing but her own mortification, Gayna pulled a disgruntled face but said nothing as she acquiescently urged the palomino forward. He might have won that round, she was forced into conceding reluctantly, but that didn't mean he'd won the war. Nor was he going to! she promised herself resolutely.

CHAPTER FIVE

'WHAT in heaven's name have you done to my hat?'
Felicity's outraged voice was the first to greet them on
their eventual return to the old homestead for lunch.

Dismounting, Gayna glanced at her with apologetic
sincerity. 'I'm very sorry, but it—er—fell off and
Prince stood on it. I'll replace it, of course,' she
offered.

'I should hope so! And not with one of inferior
quality either,' Felicity stipulated disdainfully. 'That
was a very expensive hat, I'll have you know. Although
what I'm going to wear in the meantime I have no
idea, because I certainly won't be wearing that again. I
don't intend to let my standards drop just because of
your carelessness.'

'Oh, I'm sure Gayna didn't do it on purpose,
Felicity,' interposed Raeleen on a pacifying note as she
joined them. 'Anyway, you can wear one of mine
during the rest of your stay, if you like.'

'Well, at least it will be better than wearing that
thing,' her friend accepted the suggestion ungraciously.
And to Gayna, 'If you had it on properly, I don't see
how it could have fallen off in the first place. It's not
as if you had any hard riding to do, or as if there was a
wind blowing.'

All too aware of the two men beside her, Gayna
refused to look in their direction—or Ford's, at least—
and gave a helpless shrug. 'It fell off when I fell off,'
she revealed wryly, selfconsciously. There wasn't

much point in trying to keep it a secret when she had no doubt Ford was only too anxious to regale them all with the story.

'You fell off!' Felicity promptly hooted with patent pleasure at the thought. 'You must be an even worse rider than you let on if you can't stay in the saddle on flat ground.'

'I didn't realise you'd taken a tumble,' cut in Brett, two creases of surprise appearing between his brows.

'No, well, it was while I was with Ford—after we'd split up,' Gayna began uncomfortably, and received a malevolent glare from Felicity for the information. 'I—umm . . .'

'She leant over, Prince moved unexpectedly, and the rest is history,' Ford finished for her briefly, and to her utter amazement that he hadn't disclosed the full details.

Felicity's upper lip curled into a contemptuous sneer. 'As I said, you must be even more incompetent than we realised.'

'I wouldn't exactly say that.' It was Brett who came to her defence. 'With a little more practice, I think Gayna would be your equal in no time.'

An assumption which obviously found no favour in Felicity's eyes as she haughtily sniffed, 'I doubt that very much!'

Not wanting the discussion to continue, Gayna broke in swiftly. 'Well, capable rider or not, at least I know when my mount needs a drink, so . . .' She started for the lagoon at the rear of the house, and thankful to escape—even temporarily—Felicity's derisive tongue, which she could still hear in the background.

At the lagoon's edge, standing in the mottled shade created by an enormous stand of bamboo, she let the peaceful beauty of the scene wash over her as Prince bent his head to the cool water, then turned her own head slightly on hearing other hoofs approaching, to see Ford leading both his and Brett's horse towards the pool.

For a moment she watched him covertly, chewing thoughtfully at her lip, and unconsciously noting once again the powerful width of his shoulders and the sinewed strength of his bronzed arms. She must have been mad to think she had the ability to physically force him into releasing her, she mused with whimsical self-mockery. The thought did act as a reminder, however, and she sought his attention awkwardly.

'Thank you for not disclosing the exact circumstances surrounding my fall,' she murmured almost shyly.

He gave a negligent shrug, the corners of his mouth tilting obliquely. 'I figured it was better than informing everyone of our continual disagreements.'

'I guess so,' she sighed, and made to draw Prince away from the water. She didn't want him drinking too much while he was still hot.

A hard hand coming to rest on the nape of her neck and tipping her head upwards effectively prevented her from moving any farther away. 'What's wrong, Gayna?' Ford questioned with a half smile, half frown, as his incredibly long-lashed eyes scanned her pensive features intently. 'You've gone very quiet all of a sudden. Did you let Felicity's remarks about her hat get to you?'

'No.' She shook her head gently. 'She was entitled to be annoyed. It was a very nice hat.' Avoiding looking directly at him because, unaccountably, his searching gaze was making her feel strangely confused, she laughed shakily. 'Maybe, it's just this place that's making me quiet. It's so restful I'd hate to disturb the calm.'

'Then perhaps we should do more of our talking here.'

For once Gayna didn't take exception to the slightly mocking note in his voice, but found herself, as much to her own surprise as his, laughingly agreeing, 'Perhaps we should, at that.'

Abruptly, sparkling green eyes now locked with intense blue, and the only sound that could be heard was the raucous call of a cockatoo somewhere in the trees. Then, with her heart beating a ragged tattoo against her ribs for some unknown reason, Gayna licked nervously at her lips and determinedly wrenched her gaze away.

'I—I'd better get Prince out of here before—before he drinks the lot,' she tried to joke lightly, but it had a jerky, breathless sound to it.

Ford exhaled heavily, finally freeing her, and going on to run his hand around the back of his own neck this time. 'Hmm, it probably would be advisable,' he conceded in a deeper than usual tone.

With the gelding in tow, Gayna ducked past him and hurried back to the house, her thoughts in turmoil. Good grief, whatever was the matter with her, letting him affect her to such an extent just because the serenity of the lagoon had been playing on her senses! she railed at herself vexedly as she tethered Prince in the shade at the side of the building. She would be better disposed remembering all those things she didn't like about him—goodness only knew, there were enough of them!—instead of allowing one peaceful moment of conversation to reduce her to the status of an impressionable schoolgirl! Drawing in a composing breath, her emotions well marshalled once more, she headed for the group beside the thermal pool.

Brett already had the fire going in the old stone barbecue, while Raeleen and Felicity were busy laying out cloths and bowls of food on improvised rustic tables made from rounds of sawn tree trunks. Washing her hands in the pool, Gayna dried them on a paper towel and turned to Raeleen enquiringly.

'Would you like me to do that for you?' she asked helpfully on seeing that girl beginning to slice a crusty loaf of freshly baked bread.

'If you would, please,' accepted Raeleen gratefully. 'Then I can get on with the tomatoes.' And after the younger girl had joined her on the split-log seat, 'So what did you think of your ride, and the buffalo?'

From the opposite side of the table, Felicity could hardly wait to gibe exaggeratedly, 'Not much of the ride, I expect, if she kept falling off!'

'It only happened *once*,' Gayna corrected with ironic emphasis. 'Even so, I still found the ride very interesting, as a matter of fact. The buffalo too. Although, I must admit, I don't think I'd like to face them on my own. A couple of them appeared extremely put out by our presence.'

'That's nothing to how they'll feel tomorrow,' put in Brett meaningfully.

'When you muster them?'

'Uh-huh! They get real cranky then.'

'And have you decided yet how you'll go about it? From the air, or on the ground?' Gayna asked. He and Ford had been discussing the matter on their return journey.

In lieu of answering, Brett sent a querying look over

her head and the reply came from Ford who had apparently finished watering the other two horses and
was now standing just behind his sister.

'A combination of both, I think,' he answered Brett's
unspoken question. 'We'll need the helicopter to clear
them out of the wet areas, and since Therese would
evidently like Gayna to see the mustering first
hand . . .'

'You mean you're going to take her with you?' broke
in Felicity, her expression none too pleased.

'That's right,' Ford confirmed in somewhat autocratic accents. 'Why, do you have any objections?'

'I—er—no, of course not,' Felicity denied, flustered,
and suddenly realising she might have overstepped
herself. 'It's just that I—I thought you always said you
had no time for passengers—and especially female
ones—while mustering buffalo. At least, that's what
you've always said until now!' she obviously couldn't
restrain herself from adding.

Ford returned her resentful gaze blandly. 'And until
now, that's exactly what I meant,' he advised. 'In
Therese and Gayna's cases, however . . .'

'It's purely a matter of business,' put in Gayna
decisively. She didn't want *either* of them thinking
otherwise! 'To see whether it's suitable for a tourist
attraction.'

'I thought Snow had already vetoed it as that,'
Felicity reminded her pointedly.

So he had! She'd forgotten. 'Yes, well, I haven't
actually said yet that I will be going.' In fact, if the
truth were known, she would rather not, if only to
avoid contact with Ford as much as possible.

'And now there's no need to, is there?' Felicity persisted.

'Except that, where Gayna's concerned, Ford might consider it his duty to show his future stepsister some of the operations that take place on the property,' inserted Brett whimsically.

'Mmm, that is a point.' It was his wife's turn to meditatively add her thoughts on the matter now. 'We really can't let Gayna go back to Adelaide without having seen as much as possible while she's here, can we? Business or not.'

'Perhaps Gayna's the best one to decide that,' Felicity suddenly proposed, surprisingly. 'After all, she hasn't exactly jumped at the opportunity, has she? And for someone so patently city-orientated—although, quite understandably, of course,' she added hurriedly in sugary tones, 'it may be that she's finding the prospect rather daunting, but doesn't like to say so.'

That fear might have been the reason Gayna hadn't, as yet, actually accepted the offer obviously hadn't occurred to the other three, and their glances now became doubtfully questioning as they rested on her. A circumstance which, unfortunately for Felicity, had her promptly reacting with an impetuousness equal to any her mother had ever displayed.

'Oh, no, I don't frighten that easily,' she made herself laugh lightly, albeit through somewhat gritted teeth as a result of the other girl's irritating innuendo, and refusing to be taken in by Felicity's look of pseudo-concern. 'Naturally I'd like to see how the buffalo are mustered. I just didn't want to be the cause of any extra work for anyone, that's all.'

'Right! Well, that settles that!' Brett immediately took her acceptance for granted with an approving nod. 'Now, where are those steaks, Rae? I reckon this fire's just about died down enough for them now.'

While Raeleen attended to her husband's request, Gayna set about completing her task of cutting the bread. Felicity, on the other hand, wasn't at all reconciled to the outcome of their late discussion, and as Ford moved towards the barbecue in order to give his brother-in-law a hand, she smiled cajolingly at him.

'Then if you're taking Gayna, you wouldn't mind very much if I invited myself along too, would you?' Her eyes clung to his hopefully, pleadingly. 'As you know, we're too far south for buffalo at home, and I've never seen them mustered before either.'

'Neither have you showed any interest in them before,' Brett remarked bluntly as he dropped the pieces of meat on to the hotplate one by one.

Felicity didn't even so much as blink as she continued staring soulfully at the taller man. 'Only because I knew—or thought I knew—what Ford's answer would be,' she pouted prettily.

Gayna waited with sardonic interest to hear what it would be now, and wasn't at all surprised to see him eventually flex his powerful shoulders in a gesture of careless consent.

'Under the circumstances, I guess it would be okay,' he allowed casually. 'You can go with Norm.'

Which remark had both girls staring at him in astonishment—Gayna, because she had fully expected him to revel in having the blonde's admiring company, and Felicity, because she had obviously thought the same. The older girl was the first to recover.

'Oh, but I naturally thought I'd be going with you,' she protested with a hurt look. Gayna suspected she was fuming inside, nonetheless.

'Sorry, honey, no can do. I'll have Copperknob with me,' he drawled.

'Copperknob?' Felicity puzzled.

Only just managing to recover from the knowledge that she wasn't also to be foisted on to some poor unsuspecting stockman, Gayna smiled caustically. 'I believe he means me,' she revealed, and indicating the colour of her hair. She knew all the nicknames a redhead received. 'But if you'd like to change places, I'm perfectly amenable.' Would welcome it, in fact.

'Of course I . . .'

'*Uh-uh!*' The drawl was still evident in Ford's voice as he cut in lazily, but his negation was no less forceful for all that. 'Copperknob,' which earnt him a green-eyed glare, 'comes with me. I suggested you accompany Norm, honey, because it will be less of a worry for him since, just by being raised on a cattle property, you'll be better prepared to deal with any eventuality which may occur. Gayna, of course, is nowhere near as capable in these matters,' he advised smoothly.

Felicity smiled archly at the unexpected words of praise, her expression almost gloating as it took in Gayna's less than overjoyed countenance. Little did she realise, though, that the younger girl's scowl hadn't been brought about by Ford's reference to her lack of ability—he'd spoken no more than the truth, after all—but by the manner in which he'd deliberately sweet-talked Felicity into doing exactly as he wished! It was always the same! she railed in disgust. His kind always got what they wanted because their own feelings were never deeply involved. They just played on everyone else's!

With Felicity feeling she had scored a victory, she was in a rather less malicious mood during lunch, which at least allowed the meal to be eaten in a relaxed atmosphere, and afterwards even went so far as to offer

to join Raeleen in showing Gayna over the old homestead. That was, until she discovered Ford wasn't
intending to go with them, as she had originally
thought, whereupon she promptly changed her mind
in order to avail herself of his, she hoped, undivided
attention.

Breaking off a small leaf-covered branch from a tree
as they passed Raeleen used it as a fan to keep the flies
at bay. 'Well, at least Felicity's disposition has
improved in the last hour or so,' she mused wryly as
they followed a dirt path towards the all but roofless
building. 'Although I'm sorry you had to bear the
brunt of her bad temper earlier. Goodness only knows
what was the matter with her, but thank goodness she's
not usually so—so bitchy.' Concerned brown eyes
sought Gayna's apologetically. 'I hope you didn't let
her upset you?'

Gayna shook her head briefly. 'No, she didn't worry
me,' she reassured her companion indifferently. 'Have
you known her long?'

'Just about all my life,' Raeleen laughed. 'Our fathers
have been friends ever since they were at boarding
school together.'

Mention of Lachlan had Gayna gazing at his daughter curiously, her thoughts going off at a tangent.
'What do *you* think of your father marrying my mother,
Raeleen?' she probed on a slightly tentative note. 'You
haven't said anything about it yet.'

'W-e-ll,' the word was drawn out contemplatively,
'to be honest, I was quite doubtful at first.' A rueful
smile suddenly flashed over her attractive features.
'Just like you are at the moment. But now I've become
accustomed to the idea, I really do think they'll be
very happy together.'

'I still don't see how you or—or Ford, or they for that matter, can be so certain after such a short time, though!'

Raeleen shrugged vaguely. 'Mmm, I guess it is hard to understand, but all I can say is, it's a feeling you get after seeing them together for a while. I'm sure you'll know what I mean once you've been here for a few days and spent some time with them.'

'*If* I get to spend some time with them,' qualified Gayna drily. 'The way Mum's been going so far, I'm beginning to think that's exactly what she doesn't want me to do. No sooner had I arrived than she sends me off to look over the place. Today she insisted I come out here. Tomorrow I gather I'm going to be rounding up buffalo, and after that . . . who knows?' Her mouth curved into a wry grimace. 'So just when am I supposed to see them together?'

A bubble of infectious laughter issued from Raeleen's slender throat. 'Put like that, I agree, you haven't had much of an opportunity, but I honestly don't think Therese is purposely avoiding you,' she chuckled. 'She just wants you to enjoy your stay as much as possible, that's all.'

'Yes, well, I'd be more likely to do that if I could just have a good talk with her first!'

'We'll have to see what we can arrange for the day after tomorrow, then,' suggested Raeleen with an understanding smile, leading the way on to the stone verandah surrounding the time-worn homestead.

Gayna followed slowly, her eyes taking in the pitted walls, her thoughts involuntarily slipping away from the present as her imagination tried to picture the house as it had once been—the hub of a pioneering empire.

'I wonder what it was really like in those days,' she pondered aloud.

'Lonely!' came Raeleen's laughing but explicit response. 'I understand they didn't see another white person in the first eighteen months they were here.'

Gayna frowned sympathetically. 'Perhaps that's also why they had large families . . . for company,' she suggested with a rueful half smile.

'Could be,' Raeleen granted humorously as they headed inside.

A while later, after having been guided from room to room, as well as looking over the separate kitchen quarters and storehouses, Gayna shook her head in disbelief on returning to the house once more.

'I'm not surprised your grandfather decided he needed more rooms,' she smiled. 'Where on earth did he sleep thirteen children? There just isn't that much space for them.'

'Oh, it was only the girls who had bedrooms, the boys always slept outside on the verandah,' Raeleen advised with a grin. 'Although in that regard, I must say I think the boys got the best of it.'

'Because it's cooler outside?' Gayna deduced.

Raeleen nodded so expressively they both laughed.

'So what's amusing you two?' Ford's pleasantly modulated voice suddenly broke in on their mirth from the front doorway where he leant with his upraised hands resting against the lintel.

'Nothing much,' his sister grinned, moving towards him. 'Just that you men always seem to manage to gain an advantage over us poor downtrodden females,' accompanied by a sisterly poke in the ribs as she slipped past him.

'Oh?' A cynical glance was angled in Gayna's direction as she approached him in turn. 'Do I detect a hint of your preaching there, sweetheart?'

'Not at all,' she demurred sweetly. 'Your sister just happens to be an intelligent woman. She needs no help from me to see the obvious.'

A swiftly lowered arm prevented her from following Raeleen into the sunlight, and as it curled around her lithe waist she found herself drawn relentlessly to his side.

'My sister also meant her remark as a joke,' he impressed on her mockingly.

Gayna strained away from him irritatedly. 'Well, maybe I don't consider men a joking matter!' she retorted in a tart mutter. 'So let go of me, you—you muscle-bound oaf! What did you have to come and interrupt us for, anyway?'

Ford moved his head from side to side very slowly, very definitely, and very much in warning, even though a rueful smile was playing about his lips. 'One of these days . . .!' he promised himself meaningfully.

'Yes?' she dared to challenge in defiance of her rapidly beating heart.

'Don't ask!' he recommended laconically as he removed his arm, and turning, propelled her towards Raeleen who was waiting at the edge of the verandah. 'I came to see if you were interested in joining us for a swim,' he said to his sister.

'I certainly wouldn't mind another one,' she agreed without hesitation. 'How about you, Gayna?'

Unsettled as much by Ford's dispassionate freeing of her as she had been by his disturbing capture, Gayna smiled weakly and nodded, and watched with her bottom lip caught between even white teeth as Ford began striding back down the path.

For someone who had sworn to remain cool and collected, she hadn't been very successful where Ford was concerned, she sighed dispiritedly. And the foolish part was . . . she didn't know *why* she allowed him to aggravate her so. It wasn't as if she hadn't met others of his kind before, because she had, and had no difficulty whatsoever in keeping her cool. So just what made this one different? she speculated perplexedly.

'Coming to collect your bag so we can change?' Raeleen's cheerful voice brought her out of her reverie with a slight start.

'What? Oh, yes,' Gayna recovered hastily to concur, matching her steps to the other girl's. 'Where do we change . . . in the homestead?'

'Uh-huh! Oh, and that's good, here comes Felicity now with our bags. That'll save us a walk.' Brown eyes twinkled.

'I hope you can swim better than you ride, Gayna,' tittered Felicity reaching them and handing over their appropriate carryalls.

Murmuring an acknowledgment for her bag, Gayna shrugged impassively. 'A little.'

'As long as you remember to take it easy, because as I said, they are hot springs and they can make you feel exhausted if you're not careful,' cautioned Raeleen as they retraced their steps along the path.

'You mean, like therapeutic springs?' Gayna quizzed.

'That's right,' Raeleen nodded, then quipped drily, 'That's why we're all so healthy, of course.'

At least they all certainly looked healthy, with their tanned skins, decided Gayna a while later as she emerged from the house in a low-cut, black one-piece costume made of clinging lycra with a peacock blue and white pattern running down the front. By comparison, her own winter-pale skin looked positively deathlike, she noted with a grimace.

The men were already in the pool when the girls arrived and, feeling the contrast between her paleness and their mahogany colouring was even more marked, Gayna hurriedly prepared to submerge herself in the concealing water. But not before Felicity had kindly drawn everyone's attention to her by exclaiming loudly,

'Goodness, is the "ghostly" look all the fashion down south now, Gayna?'

A pink flush of selfconsciousness tinged Gayna's cheeks as she swiftly lowered herself into the incredibly warm pool. 'No, I wouldn't exactly say it was fashionable, just unavoidable during winter,' she looked up to own drily.

'Never mind, it's no crime,' Raeleen smiled as she joined her, and sent her friend a somewhat exasperated glance. 'With that pretty red hair and those green eyes of yours, I doubt if anyone ever notices, or cares, whether your skin's tanned or not.'

'I'll endorse that!' called out Brett roguishly.

Raeleen laughed, eyeing him mock-threateningly. 'Oh, yes?'

'Only in your presence, though, my love,' he grinned in a placatory manner.

Since no one was now paying her any attention, Felicity began to make a great show of finding just the right place to dive from, and when she finally cut neatly into the water it was to coincidentally reappear immediately in front of Ford. So close in front of him, in fact, that Gayna would have been surprised if there was more than a hair's breadth between them when the blonde girl came upright.

Resting her hands against his chest, Felicity gazed up at him avidly. 'Let's have a water fight, shall we?' she suggested. 'You and I against Rae and Brett.'

Which conveniently left herself out in the cold, Gayna noticed wryly.

'Not in my condition, thanks,' Raeleen promptly reminded them of her pregnancy with a smiling shake of her head. 'Anyway, I think it would be a better idea if we cleaned the bottom of this pool. It's been a while since we were here last, and,' she winced as she took a step forward, 'it feels full of stones.' And for Gayna's benefit, 'They get washed in during the wet, so we usually try and clear them out at least once a year. As kids, we used to have competitions to see who could collect the biggest pile . . .'

'With the loser having to pack up all the picnic gear, as I recall,' inserted Ford significantly.

His sister pulled a face at him. 'What an amazing memory . . . since you only ever lost once or twice,' she retorted ruefully.

'Just a thought,' he grinned lazily.

'I think it's a good idea.' The remembrance obviously found favour in Felicity's eyes now that her suggested water fight had been summarily squashed. 'We could do the same this afternoon, provided, of course, we all keep our eyes open so we don't go blundering into each other.' She looked innocently across at Gayna. 'You can swim with your eyes open under water, I take it? I mean, I know there are a lot of people who can't.'

'Oh, I think I'll be able to manage,' Gayna replied on a sardonic note. Felicity seemed determined to fault her wherever, and whenever, possible. 'My eyes are always open,' here, she couldn't forbear sending an implicit glance in Ford's direction, 'under water, or otherwise.'

Felicity covered her disappointment with a falsely pleased smile and set about organising which areas should be reserved for their individual collections. After that, however, nothing else looked remotely organised as their mad scrambles on the bottom tended to develop into an hilarious free-for-all, complete with accusations and counter-accusations of blatant thievery, as time went on.

One such occurrence involved Gayna when, putting out her hand to retrieve a particularly large specimen, she found it suddenly whipped out from beneath her very fingertips by a larger male hand. As she had only recently done much the same to someone else, she supposed she couldn't complain, but as she was out of air in any case she rose to the surface alongside the victorious holder of what she considered to be her property.

'That was mine!' she laughed helplessly, rubbing at her eyes. They had begun to smart a little during the last few minutes.

'You've got to be quick.' It was Ford who answered so unremorsefully, causing her to drop her hands and look up in astonishment. She had been quite certain it was Brett who had poached her stone. 'There's no second prizes in this game.'

'So I learnt when your sister very smartly relieved me of some of my finds in the beginning,' she grinned.

'That sounds like Rae,' he acceded with wry humour. Then, frowning slightly, he smoothed the tip of his forefinger across her cheekbone. 'Your eyes are getting sore, aren't they?'

'A bit,' she shrugged, lightly dismissive.

'Then I guess we'd better call a halt.'

'Not while you've still got that lovely rock of mine, we won't!' she retorted, and laughing, snatched it out of his hand, intent on adding it to her own collection.

With a smothered ejaculation Ford lunged after her, his greater strength and reach giving him a decided advantage in their mirthfully punctuated struggle for possession, and his weight a telling factor when they lost their footing and sank below the water with Gayna somehow trapped beneath him. Regaining his balance first, Ford grasped her under the arms to swing her to her feet, his hands holding her firm as she coughed and spluttered on the water she'd swallowed.

Raeleen suddenly surfaced closed beside them. 'Hey! How's this for a beauty?' she exclaimed, holding out for their inspection the very stone they had just been fighting over, before turning and heading for her own pile.

'I dropped it!' explained Gayna on a part wailing, part laughing note in response to Ford's enquiringly raised brows.

'Probably on purpose,' he drawled ruefully.

'More like, in desperation! I thought you were trying to drown me.'

A fascinatingly slow smile crept over his lips which had her staring at him as if mesmerised, and her pulse beginning to pound erratically. 'Yes, well, I apologise for that,' he said. 'You did rather get the worst of it, didn't you?'

'It doesn't matter,' she discounted huskily. 'It was no doubt only what I deserved for trying to grab the stone away from you, anyway.'

'What, no recriminations for my having taken it from you first?' he puzzled in teasing tones.

Swallowing heavily, she hunched one slender shoulder in what she hoped was a sufficiently unconcerned fashion. 'It was only a game, when all's said and done.'

'And one, I might add, you were laughing about till a moment ago.'

Fortunately, the speculatively probing remark at least served to bring her back to her senses and she made herself hold his gaze defiantly. 'So? Even clowns don't laugh all the time,' she quipped, making him the butt for her annoyance with herself for once again having permitted him to get under her guard. Then, albeit not without a certain amount of relief on seeing the others all surfacing, 'It seems the others have finished now too, in any case.'

'While we leave ours for another time, hmm?'

'I don't know what you're talking about,' she denied in a studiously offhand voice, although she had her suspicions, and turning hastily, began swimming towards the other end of the pool. The finish to their constant altercations—if there was to be one—would come when she was good and ready, not before! she vowed determinedly.

Ford hauled himself agilely on to a protruding rock and walked around the pool to where Brett and his sister were already beginning to count Felicity's accumulation, with that girl keeping a sharp tally too, then continued on a few yards to lean indolently against a tree immediately above the point Gayna had chosen for her exit.

'Want a hand?' he drawled idly, proffering one, as she started to climb out. Unfortunately, there was nowhere to just walk out.

Under no illusions that his presence at that exact spot should be by accident, Gayna shot him a glowering gaze. 'No, thanks,' she refused shortly—and remembering his earlier comment regarding her capabilities, went on to snipe sardonically, 'Even if I wasn't born in the Territory, I think I can manage to at least get out of a pool on my own.'

'We'll see,' he smiled enigmatically, resuming his negligent stance.

Gayna was too occupied in levering herself upwards to bother analysing his words, and it wasn't until she was preparing to stand that the full import hit her. The warmth of the water, combined with the minerals in the pool, had made her legs feel so weak and rubbery she doubted they would support her.

'Well, you're sure taking your time about it, then.' From above her Ford's voice sounded both amused and goading.

'So don't let me keep you,' she retorted, and refusing to give him the satisfaction of seeing her attempt to stand, now presented her back to him as she slewed around into a sitting position. 'I'm just going to sit here for a while and contemplate the view.'

The next moment she was scooped effortlessly into a pair of powerful arms which pinned her to a broad chest, and found herself confronted by a pair of extremely satirical, intensely blue eyes.

'You're an obstinate little . . .!' He broke off with an incredulous shake of his head, his mouth assuming a rueful shape. 'You really like to throw down gauntlets, don't you, sweetheart?'

'No, I'd just like you to leave me alone!' she countered in a furious murmur, not wanting the others to hear. 'So would you mind putting me down!'

'Do you think you could stand?'

'Why should you care?' she rounded on him resentfully, his mocking tone doing nothing to assuage her irritation at his high-handedness, and his proximity doing nothing for her composure. 'Anyway, I was quite happy sitting where I was!'

'Especially if it provided you with an opportunity to rile me at the same time, hmm?' he surmised drily.

'Why not?' Her head lifted challengingly even as she tried to squirm free. She hated the feeling of vulnerability which always seemed to assail her at his touch. 'Do you think I don't know it was only with the idea of doing the same to me that you stationed yourself here in the first place?'

'I at least offered a helping hand,' he drawled.

And on just such a taunting note, she recalled bitterly. 'Which you knew I'd refuse!'

Ford lowered his head to close beside her ear. 'Then perhaps you should have accepted,' he murmured aggravatingly.

'And thereby surrendered to your male superiority, I suppose?' she jeered.

'And thereby avoided the contact which so obviously disturbs you to such a degree,' he amended with a mocking light in his eyes as he pointedly surveyed her stiffly held figure. Her efforts to gain release had merely proved tiring.

'Well, it's not because *you* disturb me, if that's what you're mistakenly thinking!' she blurted immediately, desperately.

'Did I say it was?' Both his eyebrows rose smoothly in unison.

Oh, God, she hadn't given herself away in her panic, had she? It would be all too humiliating if he should ever realise the demoralising effect he seemed to have on her!

'No—well—I just don't happen to be one of those females who enjoy being swept into a man's arms, that's all!' she tried to inject a little primness into her voice.

'Because you're frightened of the consequences?'

'No! Because I—because I . . . oh, for heaven's sake, put me *down*!' she ordered frantically. It was impossible to think straight while she was so aware of his warm flesh pressing against hers.

Whether Ford would have done as she'd demanded or not, Gayna never discovered, for just then Brett called from further along the pool where he and the others had been hidden from view by some intervening bushes.

'Come on, you pair! We're almost ready to start on your lot, Ford, old son.'

Now, to Gayna's utter relief, she was at last set down on the ground, and was glad to find that her legs, although still shaky, would at least support her as she promptly put a couple of steps' distance between them.

With her confidence returning, she acknowledged his action with a somewhat caustic, 'Thank you. But in future . . .'

'In future, you may not have Brett to extricate you, and then where will you be?' he interrupted tauntingly.

'Since I've never needed Brett—or anyone—to extricate me, I hardly see that it matters!'

'No? Well, I wouldn't put too much faith in that assumption, if I were you, sweetheart.'

'Meaning?' a little more warily.

'For someone who's supposed to have her emotions so securely under control, your responses sure are sus-

pect at times,' he bent his head to mock as he passed
her on his way to join the others.

A disclosure which, not unnaturally, had Gayna
staring after him in some dismay and wishing, not for
the first time, that neither she nor her mother had ever
heard of the Montgomerys!

CHAPTER SIX

IT was going on for dusk when Raeleen and Gayna finally arrived back at the main homestead after the barbecue—the others had left some time earlier and were already unsaddling at the yards as they passed—and no sooner had they pulled up at the back of the house in order to offload the picnic gear than Therese appeared on the porch with a noticeably displeased expression on her face.

'I'd like a word with you when you've finished, and before you go through into the house, please, Gayna,' she advised in her most businesslike manner as her daughter approached with one of the fridges in her hand.

Gayna both nodded and frowned her acknowledgment, continuing on into the hall with Raeleen close behind. 'I wonder what that was all about,' she turned to the smaller girl to puzzle.

'You don't think she could have had an argument with Snow, do you?' Raeleen suggested worriedly.

'No, I shouldn't think so.' It didn't take long for that idea to be vetoed by a definite shake of the head. 'I reckon she'd sound more upset if that was the case. As it is, she just sounds plain angry, and presumably with me for some reason,' came the rueful reply.

'You haven't any idea why?'

'Not a clue,' Gayna shrugged. 'She certainly seemed okay when I left this morning, and as I haven't seen her since . . . what *can* I have done to annoy her?'

It was evident from her equally perplexed demeanour that Raeleen had no explanations to offer either, although she did willingly volunteer to finish bringing in the rest of their gear on her own if Gayna wanted to find out straight away.

A proposal which was promptly declined with a wryly grimaced, 'No, thanks. I don't mind putting it off for a while. Mum doesn't often blow her top, but when she does . . .!' Green eyes rolled expressively skywards. 'She doesn't have her coloured hair for nothing, you know.'

'Yours is even more fiery than hers is,' Raeleen laughed meaningfully.

'Which could account for my more volatile temper,' Gayna conceded with a regretful grin. 'However, on this occasion I've a feeling I'm about to be on the receiving, not giving, end.'

'Well, I wish you luck, and if I can be of help in any way . . .' Raeleen allowed her words to trail away eloquently as they entered the kitchen.

From Gayna's standpoint it, unfortunately, didn't take long for the Land Rover to be emptied of its household articles, and then she was joining her mother on the porch as Raeleen re-seated herself behind the wheel in order to return the vehicle to the garage.

Therese wasted no time in getting to the heart of the matter. 'How dare you invite Alwyn here to Mundamunda!' she censured wrathfully. 'Not only is it not your prerogative to do so, but I will not be treated like a child by you two attempting to run my life for me!'

Taken aback by both the fury and content of her mother's revelation, Gayna stared at her in astonishment. 'But I—but I . . . You mean, he's coming, after all?' she stammered in confusion.

'Coming?' Therese repeated angrily. 'He *arrived* on the supply truck not half an hour ago!'

'He's here?' Gayna's eyes widened incredulously. 'But how could he be? You only rang him in Adelaide this morning, didn't you?'

'Yes, I rang him!' Therese confirmed, her seething anger almost palpable. 'He must have left as soon as he'd put the phone down . . . but without mentioning a word about his intentions to me!'

That was Alwyn, thinking he knew best again, mused Gayna glumly. 'Well, he's certainly not here at my invitation,' she put in hastily, wanting to set that matter straight at least.

'Maybe not in so many words, although you might just as well have done since the result's the same, and by your own first comment it was obvious you'd discussed the subject with him,' her mother accused.

'Well, yes, it was mentioned,' Gayna admitted uncomfortably. 'But I . . .'

'But you knew what I'd have to say about the scheme, so you also conveniently forgot to tell me, is that it?'

'No!' Gayna protested vehemently. 'He suggested accompanying me, so I told him there was no need for us both to come, and that in any case, he was needed to look after the agency because Cliff was also away.'

'Hardly what I'd call convincing, and Cliff apparently returned to work this morning.'

'Oh!' That explained Alwyn's presence.

'Is that all you've got to say?' Therese demanded, and went on without giving her a chance to answer. 'Since neither of you saw fit to warn me of the likelihood of his arrival, have you any idea how I felt on seeing him alight from that truck with a suitcase in his hand, acting like an honoured guest and all prepared for a stay? Have you?' she repeated irately. 'Well, I'll tell you. It was not only extremely embarrassing, especially when he then proceeded to tell Lachlan he's here at my daughter's invitation, but it was also too humiliating for words having everyone knowing the only reason he came was because neither of you consider me capable of making the correct decision concerning my own personal affairs!'

From the corner of her eye Gayna could see Ford nearing the house with a lithe, long-ranging stride, and although neither Brett nor Felicity were with him, luckily, that didn't stop her cheeks from burning at the thought of him overhearing her mother's stinging denunciation.

'That's not true!' she refuted Therese's claim quickly. 'We—we just don't want you making a mistake, that's all.'

'Which is just another way of saying exactly the same thing!' her mother declared, unappeased.

Gayna supposed that it was in a way. 'Well, that—that wasn't how we meant it to appear,' she tried to reassure her, and all too aware of Ford's fast closing figure. She was certain he could pick up what was being said by now. 'Anyway, surely Alwyn must have explained how . . .'

'I'm afraid I gave Alwyn very little time to explain, or indeed to say anything at all, for that matter,' Therese cut in dampeningly.

'I don't understand,' Gayna frowned.

Therese drew in a sharp breath as if just thinking about it had the power to set her smouldering. 'After his initial unasked-for remarks regarding the inadvisability of my actions—before we'd even reached the house, mind you!—I was too incensed to listen to another word and told him, without mincing matters, just what I thought of his unwarranted interference, and I haven't spoken to him since.'

Why, oh, why couldn't he have waited until they'd had a chance to talk together? 'And—er—where is he now, then?'

'Luckily for him, Lachlan has more patience than I do—he's talking to him inside—but I can tell you, Alwyn could have stayed out here until he goes back on Friday morning for all I cared!'

Never in her life had Gayna seen her mother quite so enraged, and of course it would have to have happened while Ford was around, she sighed despondently. He was only a few yards away now. Even so, she still couldn't hide her surprise at her mother's last divulgence.

'You mean, you're not letting him stay, even though he's here now?'

'That's precisely what I mean! In fact, if it wasn't for the buffalo mustering tomorrow, I would have sent him back first thing in the morning. I'm heartily sick and tired of his—and your,' she included Gayna grimly, 'unfounded insinuations and unwanted advice. So much so, I'll have you realise, that if you have any further uninvited comments to make on the matter, I recommend you go back with him as well!'

Gayna's face flamed. Not only as a result of Therese's remarks, but also because, although her mother's view of Ford might have been obscured by the flowering vine that twisted around the porch supports, hers wasn't, and she was well able to see the sardonic arching of his brows those last comments brought forth.

'You don't—you can't mean that?' she gasped throatily, disbelievingly.

On this occasion Therese's indrawn breath was more of a steadying reaction, although her expression didn't waver in the slightest. 'I do, and I can,' she stated in a voice which showed no signs of her resolve weakening. 'Alwyn's statements were just the last straw as far as I'm concerned, so if you also feel unable to accept my decision, then I'm sorry, but you leave me no choice except to say it will cause less trouble if you too return to Adelaide as soon as possible.' With which shattering bombshell she turned and walked back into the homestead.

Gayna stood as if stunned, her fingers clenching tightly at her sides, her eyes blinking rapidly at the sudden, unbidden sting of salt. God only knew what Alwyn had said to her mother, but he had certainly succeeded in putting both of them out of her favour!

'Well, you seem to have stirred up a hornets' nest this time, sweetheart,' Ford remarked casually as he stepped on to the porch. 'What brought all that on?'

Refusing to look at him, she about-faced self-consciously. 'It's none of your business!' she choked, hurriedly starting to move away.

'I beg to differ.' He caught hold of her arm to spin her back round again. 'If it happens on this property, it is my business.'

'Then go and ask my mother, I'm sure she'll be only too pleased to explain everything to your satisfaction,' she flared resentfully.

'Even if that were true, at the moment I'm asking *you*!' He determinedly tipped her face up to his.

'Why? Isn't it enough just to know that I'm leaving?'

'I wasn't aware that you were,' drily.

'Oh, don't give me that!' Momentarily, brilliant emerald eyes blazed bitterly into his, then her dark lashes lowered defensively. 'You know damned well you heard what was said! If I don't agree with her every decision, she doesn't want me around!'

'Well, that wasn't quite the way I understood it, but would that be so hard to do ... agree with her decision?' he probed.

'You already know my answer to that,' she muttered defiantly. 'I haven't changed my mind since this morning.'

'Only because you're too bloody pigheaded to!' Anger began to creep into his voice.

Even if she wasn't able to remove his grip from her arm, Gayna could at least pull her head free. 'As if you care, anyway!' she hurled back immediately. 'I've no doubt you're already jumping with joy at the thought of my impending departure. You certainly made it clear enough on the plane how unwelcome I was!'

'So what did you expect, the red carpet treatment ... after the insulting inferences you made on the phone?'

'Well, whatever the reason, it won't matter after the next couple of days, will it?' she shrugged with forced flippancy. 'I'll be gone and Mum can then concentrate on her new family to her heart's content ... as she so obviously would prefer to do!'

Ford uttered a fierce expletive. 'I ought to beat the living daylights out of you for that, you self-pitying little brat!' he threatened in a rasping tone. 'God knows why she should, but your mother thinks the sun rises and sets in you.'

'Oh, yes?' Her eyes rounded with protective facetiousness. 'Well, that's not how it sounded to me! Ordering us b-back to Adelaide just because we cared about her s-sufficiently to . . .'

'Us?' he cut in swiftly, intently.

Almost belligerently, her chin lifted a little. 'Apparently Alwyn arrived this afternoon on the supply truck.'

'At whose invitation . . . yours?' His mouth levelled ominously.

As she noted the action, her feeling of resentment grew. 'Even if I said it wasn't, you wouldn't believe me!'

'What makes you so sure of that?'

Gayna pressed her lips together vexedly and wished she'd left well enough alone.

'Because Therese didn't either?' he guessed shrewdly. 'Is that what caused the trouble between you two?'

'I told you, it's none of your business!' She refused to give him the satisfaction of a definite answer. 'And—and will you let go of my arm!' as she tried to prise open his grip. 'You're hurting me!'

'It wouldn't if you stopped fighting it,' he countered with an infuriating arrogance which had her doubling her efforts to lever his fingers apart.

'It wouldn't either if you just let go!' she retaliated acidly. 'Or is this how you get your kicks? By using brute force on females?'

'With you, I don't appear to have much option,' he relayed just as caustically. 'It's the only way in which I can make certain you won't go running off at the first opportunity.'

'You could always try taking the hint that I have

absolutely no desire to talk to you,' she suggested with pseudo-sweetness.

'Mmm, I could,' he conceded lazily, 'but then I'd never discover just what's going on in that pretty head of yours, would I?'

The unexpected compliment threw her off balance for a second, surprising her into halting her attempts to gain her liberty. 'Don't tell me you're interested,' she scoffed.

'Only in so much as it affects this property and the people on it,' she was informed in a sardonic drawl as his black-framed eyes roamed over her upturned features with leisurely thoroughness. 'Or were you hoping there was another, more personal, reason?'

'Don't be ridiculous!' Her denial came tumbling out in a strangled voice, due as much to that discomposing gaze as to his words.

'Then there should be nothing to prevent us from conducting a perfectly rational conversation without you behaving like a frightened rabbit, should there?' One well-shaped brow rose whimsically.

'I'm not frightened of you, Ford Montgomery, if that's what you're trying to imply!' she burst out hotly. Annoyingly, he had the uncanny knack of continually being able to put her on the defensive. 'I just take extremely strong exception to discussing private family matters with strangers, that's all.'

'Strangers?' he repeated on a dry note. 'Sweetheart, whether you approve of the idea or not, before very long we're going to be related, and so whatever concerns you and your mother from here on concerns my family too.'

The fact that he was probably right didn't make her feel any happier, or more ready to accept the situation, but determined not to give him the chance to level that charge of 'frightened rabbit' at her again, she took a deep stabilising breath and eyed him unflinchingly.

'Only in some instances,' was all she would allow even so.

A wry half smile pulled at the corners of his mouth in recognition of her obvious reluctance. 'Of which this happens to be one.'

'All right, of which this happens to be one!' she heaved defeatedly. Since Alwyn had invited himself into the Montgomery's home, she guessed she could hardly continue to dispute the matter. Then, to ensure the victory wasn't all his, she asked mockingly, 'Now may I have my arm back?'

'Are you intending to stick around?' His response was no less tauntingly made.

'I wasn't aware I had a choice.'

'You don't.'

She hadn't expected otherwise. 'Since you put it like that, then I suppose I will be staying, won't I?' she half quipped, half grimaced.

'I knew you'd see it my way,' he grinned, at last relinquishing his hold.

Against her will Gayna laughed, her pearly white teeth shining as her mouth shaped wryly. 'You're all heart!'

'And you . . .' resting his fingers lightly beneath her chin, his thumb gently traced the contours of her soft lower lip, 'should laugh more often.'

Mesmerised for the moment, she could only stare at him helplessly, then re-gathering her senses she averted her face as a tide of rosy colour steadily mounted her petal-smooth cheeks. 'Yes—well—some other time, maybe,' she stammered on a thickening note. 'Of late, I'm afraid I haven't found much to laugh about.'

'And especially not this afternoon, hmm?'

A particular timbre in his tone had her wondering whether he wasn't also meaning with regard to himself at the pool, as well as her confrontation with her mother, but either way she felt her answer was appropriate as she shrugged with as much unconcern as possible and granted, 'You could say that.'

'Due solely to Alwyn's arrival?' His blue eyes held hers watchfully.

'So it would seem.'

Ford's expression became even more alert. '*Did* you invite him to Mundamunda?' he probed.

'No,' she denied flatly.

'Yet Therese didn't believe you, apparently.'

'It wasn't so much that she disbelieved me, as that she appears to consider I could have voiced stronger objections when he suggested the idea,' she relayed with a sigh.

'Why didn't you, then? Because, if the truth was known, you did actually want him to come?'

'No, not really.' She shook her head slowly, her mood meditative. 'I think I figured that if I couldn't get Mum to—to change her mind, then there wasn't much likelihood of his being able to. As for the other,' she gave a rueful half laugh, spreading her hands graphicly wide, 'well, I thought I had put forward suitable objections to his coming.'

Ford thrust his hands into the back pockets of his pants, his eyes narrowing with a frown. 'And that was sufficient to have Therese hauling you over the coals?'

'She said it was just the last straw,' Gayna explained sombrely, eyes downcast as she studied the toes of her dusty sneakers. 'Apparently she was pretty embarrassed and annoyed just to see Alwyn turn up, but when he not only told your father that he was here at my invitation, but also immediately proceeded to give her a lecture . . .' She hunched her shoulders fatalistically in an effort to camouflage her hurt. 'I guess she thought she might as well dispose of all her opposition in one fell swoop by recommending I return to Adelaide too.'

'Except that, in your case, it *was* only a recommendation, not an order,' he emphasised significantly.

Gayna gave a brittle, mirthless laugh. 'Mmm, provided I make no more comments regarding her decision. An ultimatum she was well aware I wouldn't—couldn't—accept!'

'And did you bother to stop and think how distressing it must have been for her to make such a statement?'

Uncaring of the tightening tone of his voice, she burst out bitterly, 'Probably about as much as the thought she gave for my feelings in making it so painfully obvious that she doesn't need me any more now that she has the Montgomerys making such a fuss over her! Well, if that's the way she wants it, then . . .'

'That's not the way she damned well wants it, and you know it!' he cut in peremptorily. 'And nor will you be leaving with this Alwyn, so you can scrap that idea as soon as you like.'

'Can I? That's what you think!' she promptly flouted. 'I'm not staying here after . . .'

'Oh, yes you are!' he interrupted again to contradict in the same arbitrary manner.

'No, I am not! Mum made it quite clear . . .'

'That your opposition is tearing her apart!' he interjected for the third time, but with more anger evident on this occasion. 'Or is it that you just don't care?'

'You've got no right to say that!' she defended resentfully. 'It is only because I care that I came in the first place!'

His blue eyes raked over her derisively. 'But, as usual, you'd rather run once the going gets rough, huh?'

'Like my father, is that what you're trying to say?' she deduced on a taut, bitter note.

Ford inclined his head in a satirically acknowledging gesture. 'It would appear there are similarities.'

If he had thought to disconcert her as much as he had when he'd made such a comparison previously, Gayna vowed to herself that he'd be disappointed this time, and although her shallow breathing was somewhat erratic, she at least made certain her return gaze was steady.

'Then I've no doubt she'll be as pleased to see the last of me as she was of him!' she asserted with feigned indifference.

'Uh-uh!' he disallowed sardonically, waving a censuring finger at her. 'You're not squirming out of it that easily, sweetheart. As I said, *you're staying,* like it or not! It's time someone made you see the world as it really is, and . . .' he caught her chin between thumb and finger, 'you're going to make amends Therese.'

Gayna broke away from him furiously, his dictates grating intolerably. '*I'm* going to make amends?' she echoed incredulously. 'All I did was to get out of the car and then I was being blown sky-high! And I can see the world for what it is quite nicely without any doubtful assistance from you, thanks all the same!'

'You surprise me,' he drawled laconically. 'I wouldn't have thought your head was ever out of the sand long enough for you to see anything.'

'Is that so? Well, for your information, there's quite a few things about me that would probably surprise you, Ford Montgomery!' she gibed tartly.

'Sounds intriguing. Another reason for making certain you stay around for a while longer, perhaps?' One dark brow crooked in taunting speculation.

So that he might analyse her every move and reaction like some scientist probing for a new discovery? Not if she could help it! He was causing her enough problems already, one way or another, without being subjected to that.

'I only said you might be *surprised* . . . not that you would be *interested*,' she stressed with what she hoped was the right amount of faintly mocking amusement.

'You don't think I'd be the best judge of that?'

He was deliberately baiting her and she changed her stance restively beneath his knowing gaze.

'Possibly,' she allowed with a dismaying nervousness, but hastened to add, 'Although not necessarily, of course.'

'No, of course not,' he concurred, but so drily that she didn't dare even think of relaxing her guard. Then he suddenly smiled, as if well aware of her inward turmoil, and all too attractively for Gayna's peace of mind. 'But for now, I might suggest you introduce me to this Alwyn of yours while there's still time before dinner.'

Thankful at least for the diversion of his interest, she promptly disclaimed, 'He's not *my* Alwyn! If he's anyone's, he's my mother's, and you don't need me to introduce you, anyway. Since I understand he's talking to your father, Lachlan should be able to do that for you.'

Apart from her own desire to escape Ford's disturbing company, she had a strong premonition that he and Alwyn were two men who were never likely to see eye-to-eye, and in consequence she had no wish to witness their meeting—and especially not under the prevailing circumstances!

'You preferring to run away again, is that it?'

'No,' she denied hastily, albeit somewhat guiltily. This time she supposed he was right in a way, although she would rather have described her reluctance to go with him as discretionary more than cowardly. 'I just didn't want to become even more involved, that's all.'

'Well, whether you want to be or not, you already are involved, Copperknob, make no mistake about that . . . and right up to your slender little neck!' he advised with a wryly sardonic inflection. 'Besides, don't you think you owe it to him to at least go and greet him?'

'I was going to as soon as I'd showered and changed,' she justified. It wasn't Alwyn she was trying to avoid! 'And don't call me Copperknob!' she continued on a much less defensive note. 'I dislike that sort of nickname intensely.'

'Although "sweetheart" is acceptable, I presume, since you haven't objected to that so far?' lazily.

'That—that's different,' she stammered selfconsciously, her cheeks becoming suffused with colour. 'It's not a nickname, it's a—a . . .'

'An endearment?' he mocked.

The stain covering her cheeks darkened uncontrollably. 'Not the way you usually say it. Then, it's more like a sarcasm,' she countered with protective astringency.

Ford's eyes gleamed with a humorous light. 'Never!' he denied drolly.

Gayna dropped her own gaze in confusion. 'Yes, well, if you've finished making fun of me, shouldn't we be going inside? That is, if it is still your intention to meet Alwyn before dinner.' She tried to instil a little firmness into her voice at least.

'Oh, that's my intention all right,' he drawled. 'But now you're anxious to see him, are you?'

'Not particularly,' she shrugged, and doing her best to ignore the implicit taunt contained in his words. 'It is getting late, though.' The nightly chorus of clicking, whirring insects was already under way.

'So it is,' he smiled whimsically. 'And as you say, the—er—estimable Alwyn awaits.'

Gayna let that pass without comment. Although it did make her even more apprehensive in one regard. Ford obviously wasn't feeling particularly well disposed towards her mother's manager already!

When Alwyn strolled out on to the verandah after dinner, Gayna promptly followed him through the french doors because it was the first opportunity she'd had of speaking to him alone.

'What in heaven's name did you say to Mum when you arrived this afternoon that made her erupt in such a fashion?' she demanded immediately she was certain they were out of earshot of the others.

Alwyn's mousy-coloured brows lifted as if in surprise. 'Only that I considered her decision to be both ill-conceived and ill-timed.'

'Only!' she part gasped, part choked in dismay. 'Couldn't you at least have waited till you'd spoken to me about it, instead of sermonising the minute you set

foot on the place? Now all you've done is to ruin whatever chance either of us had of changing her mind.'

'All I did was to tell her what I thought of the idea,
and that wouldn't have altered no matter when I spoke
to her,' he declared somewhat huffily. 'Anyway, you
don't seem to have made much impression on her since
you've been here, although I suppose that's not so surprising since I arrived to find you've been out on a
picnic all day.' His eyes half-closed suspiciously. 'What
progress did you hope to make that way? A liaison of
your own with that autocratic bastard, the son and
heir?'

'Oh, don't be so damned ridiculous!' she flared, and
only just managing to hold on to her temper. After all,
his meeting with Ford before dinner *had* been as
fraught with tension and undercurrents as she had suspected would be the case. 'The only reason I went was
because I wasn't really given a choice in the matter.
The same as for this buffalo muster they've got on
tomorrow. And while we're on the subject of progress
. . . at least Mum was still talking to me before you
arrived! She isn't any more, thanks very much!'

'Well, how was I to know she was going to fly off
the handle like that? She usually welcomes my opinion.'

'In matters of business, maybe, but this happens to
be somewhat different. Or hadn't you noticed that
small fact?'

'If I hadn't, being sarcastic certainly isn't going to
help,' he retorted in an acrimonious tone.

'At this stage, do you know anything that is?' Gayna
grimaced.

Exhaling heavily, a disgruntled expression settled on
his thin features. 'Not since Therese suggested—or

should I say, commanded?—I join you on this blasted hunt tomorrow. I could have done without that, I can tell you!'

'Then perhaps you shouldn't have been quite so disdainful about the matter when it was mentioned during dinner,' she put forward wryly. 'You know it's been a pet project of hers for some time now.'

'But not to the extent where I'd be expected to physically take part in it, I didn't,' he complained. 'Good grief, she knows dashing about the bush in a four-wheel-drive isn't my style!' The corners of his mouth took a derisive turn downward. 'I prefer to leave that to the beefy types who like to think it gives them a tough image.'

Gayna suspected that last gibe had been aimed at Ford, but refrained from voicing her thoughts that where he and Brett were concerned, she had the feeling that the aura of virile strength they both exuded wasn't an image at all, but fact!

Instead, she proposed ruefully, 'Mum also knows that if we're both out there somewhere,' gesturing into the distance, 'then we can't be here trying to change her mind, can we?'

'You mean, you think it's merely an excuse to get us both out of the way?' he sought her confirmation in a shocked tone.

'I'd say it was more than a possibility,' she shrugged philosophically.

Alwyn's yellow-brown eyes scrutinised her sharply. 'Well, you certainly don't sound very upset about it!' he accused.

'Probably because I'm beginning to think we're pursuing a lost cause,' she sighed. 'It would seem Mum has made up her mind she's going to marry Lachlan and nothing we say or do is going to stop her.'

'And the agency? What's going to happen about that, then?' he enquired sharply. 'Or doesn't she care any more now that she's fallen on her feet?'

'Of course she cares, otherwise she wouldn't still be trying to finalise accommodation arrangements for these homestead/wildlife tours she's so keen on. Anyway, what do you mean, now that she's fallen on her feet?' she demanded with some asperity. She hadn't liked the rather sneering tone he'd used.

'It's obvious, isn't it?' he countered, and this time his cynicism was quite open. 'I started making some enquiries re the Montgomerys yesterday—as we'd arranged—and, believe me, it wasn't long before the pieces began falling into place.'

'Meaning?'

'That the joke's on us, naturally! Lachlan Montgomery isn't marrying Therese for whatever money she possesses. It's the other way around,' he propounded pungently.

Gayna stared at him wrathfully. It was bad enough that Felicity had made such an assumption, but that Alwyn should too made her twice as furious. 'How dare you! Mum would never do such a thing!' she defended hotly. 'She's in love with Lachlan . . . or thinks she is,' honesty forced her into adding, but grudgingly.

'And the fact that the family just happens to be rolling in money has nothing to do with it, I suppose?' His mouth curved sarcastically. 'Come off it, Gayna, I didn't think you were that naïve! Of course Therese is feathering her nest while she's got the opportunity. Why else do you think she refuses to even talk about the subject? Because she doesn't want us to suspect, that's why! And it's precisely for that reason that I spent the afternoon being bounced around in that infernal semi-trailer ... because I can see her disposing of the agency—without a thought for our verbal agreement—just so she can look the part of the wealthy widow and thereby put everyone off the scent.'

'How can you even think such a thing?' she rounded on him, shocked. 'Although that's all you're concerned about, isn't it? The damned agency! You couldn't care less whether she's likely to be happy or not. No, you're only worried in case *your* plans are upset in some way!'

'Not entirely,' he denied, but without quite meeting her fierce gaze. 'I *do* think her action is precipitate and extremely impulsive, but at the same time, I also feel I have an obligation to us to fulfil.'

'To us?' Gayna queried with a frown.

'It's not only my livelihood I'm thinking about, it's yours too, you know,' he smiled ingratiatingly.

'Oh, yes?' Gayna's voice registered her total disbelief. 'And why should you feel any concern about my livelihood?'

'Well, I know how hard you've worked to help Therese build the agency up to what it is today, and,' Alwyn moved closer to murmur in a suavely confidential tone, 'as you've come to mean quite a lot to me over the last few months, I was hoping ...'

'Yes?' she prompted coolly, as cold now as she had previously been hot.

'I was hoping that if you and I—shall we say, got together?—then perhaps Therese might like to retire, and we could run the agency together,' he suggested with unctuous persuasiveness.

An icy anger began to spread through Gayna's veins. Having had the effrontery to accuse her mother of being nothing more than a gold-digger, he now had the presumption to think she was going to fall into his lap like a ripe apple!

'And that way you wouldn't be called upon to pay out any money in order to get your hands on the business, would you?' she bit out contemptuously.

Two dark blotches of colour appeared high on his cheekbones. 'No, you misunderstand me,' he tried to impress on her urgently. 'It's you I'm thinking of. Your welfare, your happiness.' Abruptly, his emotions seemed to get the better of him and, grasping her arms, he pulled her to him roughly. 'You must believe me! I haven't said anything before because I didn't think the time was right, but it's not just the agency . . . it's you I really want! I can't get you out of my mind these days, and whenever I'm with you it's like I'm on fire inside,' he vowed hoarsely as he bent his head towards hers.

Unmoved by what she considered, knew, to be his calculated appeal to her feelings, Gayna strained stiffly away from his descending head and with her hands flat against his chest gave him a shove that sent him staggering backwards into the verandah rail.

'Then I recommend you take a cold shower to douse the flames!' she quipped sarcastically as she stormed past him.

'Because you're holding out for bigger fish?' he insinuated with a malevolent sneer.

How little he knew her! Half turning, she fixed him with a pitying glance. 'At least that would be preferable to settling for an overly ambitious toad,' she informed him, sweetly scornful, and continued on her way.

Of course, it would also be preferable if she could remain as unstirred when dealing with one other particular male, she mused pensively—then consoled her-

self with the thought that since she had known Alwyn
so much longer, it was probably only a matter of time
before familiarity provided her with the same immunity against Ford.

CHAPTER SEVEN

THE sun was only just rising when they set off the following morning, the helicopter with Brett at the controls sounding abnormally loud in the still, cool air, and sending a myriad birds aloft in an added cacophony of complaints as it interrupted the last of their sleep.

For those on the ground, three old converted Land Rovers—their cabins removed and replaced with rollbars—provided the transport and, dressed as advised in her oldest pair of denims and a check shirt, with Felicity's damaged hat on her head—that girl having borrowed a more respectable one from Raeleen—Gayna climbed gingerly on to the dusty seat of the lead vehicle. Behind her, Felicity and Alwyn were doing likewise. Felicity with simpering exclamations of excitement, and Alwyn with obvious disinclination.

Their drivers, two stockmen by the names of Norm and Athol, were wearing faded drill shirts and shorts, as was Ford, their feet covered by strong leather boots with heavy woollen socks folded down over the tops. A fourth vehicle containing three other similarly clad men had already been despatched on ahead.

'All set?' enquired Ford as he took the seat beside her after whistling up two of the ever-present cattle dogs into the back of the small truck.

'I guess so,' she allowed with a shrug.

Leaning forward slightly to switch on the ignition, he slanted her a wry sidelong glance. 'Well, don't sound so enthusiastic about it, you might accidentally find yourself becoming interested,' he charged drily.

As usual, where he was concerned, what little control she did have immediately fled. 'I happen to have a lot on my mind!' she flared excusingly.

'With regard to Therese, or,' nodding over his shoulder, 'the master of discordance, back there?'

Certainly not Alwyn, that was for sure! Not after his obnoxious accusations concerning her mother. His sly attempt to gain control of the agency through herself she had already contemptuously dismissed out of hand.

'My mother, of course,' she answered as if it should have been a foregone conclusion. 'She as good as cut me dead at dinner last night.'

'Well, you must admit friend Alwyn wasn't helping matters any with his continual dissension,' Ford drawled as he started the vehicle moving.

'So why should I get the blame for what he says?' resentfully.

'Probably because Therese sees you as two minds with but a single thought . . . to stop her marriage at any cost!'

Gayna shifted uncomfortably on the seat. 'Yes—well—even so, I still think it's unfair of her to credit me with exactly the same sentiments as Alwyn,' she complained a little sulkily.

'Aren't they?' One of his brows quirked half humorously.

'No! He's only interested in . . .!' She came to an abrupt halt, suddenly aware that she was saying too much and considering it none of his business. 'Well, it doesn't matter what he's interested in,' she went on with an offhand hunching of her shoulders. 'Let's just say he doesn't speak for both of us, that's all.'

'I see.' Although Ford kept his eyes to the front, it was still possible to see the corners of his shapely mouth pulling sardonically upwards. 'And just what made you come to the startling, but entirely predictable, conclusion that Mr Carson's only interest in the matter was the effect it would have on his own ambitions, hmm?'

'How did you know?' The partly suspicious, partly surprised words burst out before she could stop them.

'Therese thought that might be the case all along,' he supplied idly.

'She discussed it with *you?*'

'And Snow.'

'But not with me, I note,' she observed somewhat bitterly.

Ford spared her a quizzical look. 'Would you have been particularly receptive, if she had?'

Gayna couldn't really answer with any certainty, but . . . 'She could at least have given me the benefit of the doubt! Or is it only the Montgomerys' opinions she's interested in these days?'

'Would you blame her?' he countered with an ironic half laugh. 'You're so one-eyed about the whole thing you refuse to even see the obvious, let alone admit it.'

'Only according to you!'

'And Therese, apparently.'

The cutting retort had Gayna biting hard at her lip and averting her head quickly lest he see just how deeply his thrust had penetrated. The fact that he seemed to be speaking the truth made it no easier to bear.

Beside her, Ford rubbed distractedly at his forehead and released a heavy breath. 'I'm sorry, I shouldn't have said that,' he apologised in a rough-edged tone.

'It doesn't matter,' she disclaimed huskily with a brief shake of her head. 'Why should you apologise for telling the truth?'

'Because it was both unwarranted and unnecessary.'

'Oh, well, at least it got your message across,' she attempted to laugh nonchalantly, but when it didn't succeed lapsed into selfconscious silence.

Ford muttered a succinct epithet and flicked her an exasperated glance. 'God, you're a contradiction!' he denounced gruffly.

Astonishment had Gayna swinging to face him again, but only momentarily, and then she was resuming her defensively evasive pose once more. The indefinable expression in his eyes only added to her confusion.

'Look who's talking!' she gibed shakily. 'If I didn't know better, I might almost be persuaded into thinking . . .'

'Mmm?' he cued wryly, expectantly.

'It's not important,' she shrugged, and realising they were travelling on a different track from the one they had taken the day before, thankfully took the opportunity to change the subject by asking, 'Aren't we going through the valley today?'

In the short silence which followed, Gayna wondered apprehensively if he intended pressing for her to continue what she had started to say, but eventually she was able to sigh with relief on hearing him advise, 'No, Brett'll clear them out of there in the chopper better than we could. We're detouring around the southern arm of the valley and will pick them up as they emerge on to the plains.'

'Then where do you take them?' she queried, not wanting the conversation to flag.

'North. We've some yards hidden in the thickest part of the scrub out there. That's where the other truck went—to make everything ready.'

'And once you've got them yarded?'

'They're culled, any young ones we decide to keep being brought back to the homestead, the rest shipped out to the abattoir.' He sent her a lazily speculative look. 'Anything else?'

'Yes,' she confirmed hurriedly, trying to ignore the wayward leap of her senses in response to that disconcerting gaze. 'Why are the yards hidden in the scrub? Wouldn't it be easier to herd them all in if they were out in the open?'

'Uh-uh!' he drawled, shaking his head. 'Not only are the yards then camouflaged, but buffalo instinctively head for the scrub thinking it to be their best chance of escaping. Out in the open you've got the devil's own job to keep them from breaking in all directions.'

'Why is why you need three vehicles?' she guessed.

'Too right,' he acknowledged laconically. 'One on each flank, one at the rear, and the chopper overhead to keep 'em moving.' He suddenly started to laugh, ruefully. 'And even then they can make things chancy at times!'

'By charging?' She remembered Brett saying something similar yesterday. Then, as her vision involuntarily focussed on the heavy steel bull-bar on the front of the truck, gulped somewhat less blithely, '*Us?*'

'Uh-huh!'

All of a sudden Gayna became very much aware of the gaping space beside her where once a door had been. 'If one of them comes up on this side . . .' She shivered expressively.

'Then we could both find ourselves in trouble,' Ford relayed ironically. 'Side on, they can turn one of these over with very little effort at all.'

'Oh, fantastic! That really makes me feel better,' she grimaced with hollow humour. 'Are you sure this is the same vehicle you took my mother out in, or have you removed the doors just for me?'

'No, it's the same,' he grinned wryly. 'But just to relieve your mind, I'll have you know it's my job to see they only get to charge the front of the truck, not the sides.'

'Hmm, but the question is, are you any good at your job?' she quipped in mocking tones.

'I'm still here, aren't I?' he countered with a laugh.

'That's true,' she allowed, nodding, and followed it with a dulcetly smiled, 'But can the same be said of your previous passengers, that's what I'd like to know.'

'Your mother was one,' he reminded her on an easy note.

'And the others?'

'Don't worry, the few there have been were none the worse for wear afterwards ... once their broken bones had mended, of course.'

Although she strongly suspected he was only paying her back in kind, from his bland expression Gayna couldn't be quite certain and, in consequence, hazarded tentatively, 'You're joking ... I hope?'

At first, all Ford would do was to flex his broad shoulders noncommittally, but on seeing her forehead begin to furrow with lines of doubt, relented and endorsed, 'You're right, I'm joking.' His thickly lashed eyes met hers briefly, seriously. 'Although I'm not joking when I say it *can* be dangerous, so make sure you hold on tight once we start chasing, okay?'

Gayna nodded her agreement obediently, realising he was in earnest now. 'A limpet will have nothing on me, I can assure you,' she told him explicitly.

Soon, the character of the country they were travelling across began to alter, becoming flatter and more open, the trees more widely spaced, and allowing for the first time occasional glimpses of grey-coated cattle grazing the vast grasslands. Gayna drank it all in appreciatively. There was that to be said for the outback, she mused whimsically. It was incredibly peaceful. At least, it was now that the helicopter had left them, she amended with an inward smile.

Leaning farther back in her seat, she found her thoughts wandering on, her eyes somehow irresistibly, covertly, drawn to the profile of the man beside her. With his own eyes narrowed against the onrushing air—there were no windscreens on these vehicles—he appeared so wholly engrossed in what he was doing that it startled her to abruptly find herself receiving a silent enquiry in the form of arching brows as his deep blue eyes encountered hers transiently, and for all the world as if he had immediately sensed her surreptitious scrutiny.

'I was just wondering,' she began selfconsciously, but feeling she had to justify her examination of him somehow. 'Did you ever suspect my mother might be marrying your father for *his* money, Ford?' Since the reverse had been her initial thought on the matter, and resurrected by Alwyn's recent charges, it was a question which had been in her mind only minutes before.

For his part, Ford's reaction caught her completely unprepared, however, and she stared at him in wide-eyed dismay to hear him condemn scathingly, 'You contemptible little bitch! You're willing to say absolutely anything—even discredit your own mother—in order to get your way, aren't you?'

'No!' she protested hoarsely. 'You've got it all wrong!'

'I'll bet!'

'But you have!' she insisted. 'I wasn't trying to imply that was the reason she's marrying Lachlan.'

'Weren't you?' His mouth shaped sardonically.

'No, I wasn't!' she smouldered in return, an angry indignation sweeping over her. 'As much as this may come as a surprise to you, but I happen to think far too much of my mother to even contemplate denigrating her in such a fashion, no matter what the circumstances! I didn't say she *was* marrying Lachlan for his money, I merely asked if *you* had ever suspected she might be doing so!'

'Then the answer to that is, no! It's been obvious to all but the deliberately blind just why she's marrying him right from the beginning,' he retaliated bitingly, and certainly with no less hostility. 'But don't you start venting your resentment on me, sweetheart, because you've got no one else but yourself to blame if everyone believes the worst of you. You've made it abundantly clear, ever since Therese telephoned you, that you're prepared to forward any argument—no matter how depreciating—as long as it might have a chance of separating those two, so don't start complaining now that you're reaping what your prejudices have sown!'

He made her position sound indefensible, and yet ... she hadn't been entirely wrong, had she? She had only wanted to protect her mother, after all. Admittedly, she perhaps shouldn't have allowed her feelings such full rein, but at the same time that call had come as something of a shock, and when she re-membered her mother's previous remarks concerning remarriage, well, was it really any wonder that her sus-picions had been aroused?

Not that Ford seemed to think she was entitled to doubts of any kind, she noticed morosely, for his ex-pression was as formidable now as it had been when he'd flown her to Mundamunda, and strangely, that made her feel most dispirited of all. Why it should be that way she wasn't even able to give herself a satisfac-tory reason, unless of course it was just because she was unaccustomed to having her actions so summarily condemned and misconstrued.

'As a matter of fact, I was only saying to Alwyn last night that—that I thought we were pursuing a lost cause,' she offered hesitantly in a small voice, hoping for perhaps a change in his demeanour.

There was none forthcoming, though, as he retorted in heavily sarcastic tones, 'That was extremely mag-nanimous of you!'

'Well, I wasn't meaning to be,' she refuted diffi-dently. 'I was just trying to explain . . .'

'What?' he cut in to prompt harshly. 'That as Therese had made it plain she didn't intend listening to any more of your objections, you were only just beginning to realise how serious she was about the matter, but that you'd rather break her heart by refus-ing to say as much because that would mean having to admit you'd been wrong?'

Gayna's eyes misted. 'Is that what you really think? That I won't agree with Mum out of spite?' she quest-ioned with a stricken catch in her voice.

Ford gave an dispassionate shrug. 'So it would seem.'

The mist threatened to become a flood and she wiped the back of her hand hastily across her eyes. 'Well, I guess that's telling me,' she half choked on the attempted flippancy. 'I should have known better than to lead with my chin, shouldn't I?'

Ford shot her an encompassing glance which connected with a shimmering emerald gaze and then he was dragging a hand irritably around the back of his neck. 'Oh, hell!' he cursed. 'Will you stop keep looking like a child who doesn't know why it's being punished!'

'Then don't keep treating me like one! I was in primary school the last time I acted out of spite!' she cried.

His lips twitched wryly and then stilled. 'Okay, so if that isn't the reason, would you mind telling me what in damnation is?'

'I already have. You just choose not to believe me,' she sighed dejectedly.

'You can't mean . . .'

'Yes, I can,' she interposed, knowing precisely what he was going to say. 'It—it's insanely impulsive for either of them to be considering marriage after such a short time.'

'Hmm, but then you don't exactly have a good opinion of men, or marriage, under any circumstances, do you?' ironically.

'That has nothing to do with it,' she contended, albeit flushing slightly.

A grudging smile caught at the edges of his firm mouth, making it more attractive than ever. 'You don't think it may be colouring your attitude to some extent?'

Gayna swallowed convulsively to remove the lump

which seemed to have lodged in her throat. 'No,' she denied thickly. 'As it so happens, I—I like your father.' An admission that came as a surprise even to herself. 'So if Mum's going to remarry, I would as soon it was to him as anyone else.'

'Well, I suppose that's something.' The upward curve of his lips became more wryly pronounced. 'And is the length of time they've known each other your only objection?'

'N-o,' she drew the word out carefully. 'I think consideration should also be given to whether Mum will be able to adapt to living in the outback after leading such a busy life in the city. Not everyone could, you know.'

'Meaning, you couldn't?'

'I—well—it would all depend on the circumstances, I guess.' Which was something else she had never expected to hear herself say. Perhaps the serenity of her surroundings was getting to her again, the same as it had at the lagoon behind the old homestead. 'I've never thought I would, but then I've never tried either,' she shrugged.

'Then you will no doubt be relieved to know that Therese says she's thoroughly looking forward to it.'

'She is?' Gayna couldn't keep the amazement out of her voice. Her mother had never expressed a wish to live anywhere else but in the city before. Of course, things were slightly different now, but even so . . . 'Well, I expect it's something of a novelty for her at the moment.'

For some reason Ford seemed to find that amusing. 'Oh, sweetheart, you're unreal!' he laughed ruefully.

'Because I prefer to weigh all the pros and cons?' she asked, stiffening.

'Because you're so determined to find obstacles,' he countered drily. 'Why don't you just relax and let Therese and Snow worry about their own problems, if and when they occur, huh? You act as if she's *your* daughter, instead of it being the other way around.'

'But we've always sought each other's opinion on important matters,' she defended quickly, if a trifle embarrassedly. He made her feel like a finicky maiden aunt. 'Don't you talk things over with Lachlan too?'

'Not on subjects of a personal nature, no. I figure he's old enough to both make up, and know, his own mind ... and to solve his own mistakes, should he make any.'

'I see,' she nodded dismally. Then, more purposefully after a moment's thought, 'But if I don't say anything, and it doesn't work out, she'll ...'

'Gayna!' he cut in with a mixture of exasperation and disbelief. 'Will you forget all that for the moment, and just answer me one question?'

'What sort of question?' A wary expression clouded her features.

'A very pertinent one, I think you'll find,' he disclosed in a drawl. 'And that is, are you certain Therese did actually *ask* for your opinion on this occasion?'

Temporarily, silence reigned as the full implication of his enquiry swept over her, and as she thought back frantically over her conversations with her mother. She must have done, surely! They always discussed matters which concerned them both.

'Well?' urged Ford softly.

'No, I don't think she did,' she conceded finally with a hint of both bewilderment and despondency in her tone.

'A fair indication of the strength of her feelings in

the matter, wouldn't you say?' he proposed, gently insistent.

'I guess so.' Her concurrence was reluctantly given.

It was depressing to discover her views were suddenly no longer wanted, and it made her realise just how far apart her mother's life would be from her own in future. Not that she had any desire to deliberate that particular aspect with Ford, though, and she cast about desperately for a suitable change in topic.

Fortunately, by then they had almost reached the end of the valley where it met the grasslands they were traversing before spreading into the far-reaching red soil plains, and all at once the whirring throb of the helicopter carried clearly to them on the still air.

'It sounds as if we've only just made it in time,' it enabled her to exclaim.

'No, he's still a way distant yet,' Ford corrected, but with such a dry inflection in his tone that she was positive he was aware of her intention.

'So what do we do now, then . . . wait?' she rushed on. It looked to her as if they were almost to the centre of the valley's mouth already.

'Shortly,' he advised. 'I want us stationed a bit farther north when Brett brings them out, in the hopes of preventing them from heading in among those paperbacks,' indicating a swampy area to their right thickly covered with slender white-trunked trees.

'What would happen if they did get in there?'

'We might not get them all out again, but we'd have a hell of a long wait while Brett tried.'

'Oh!' she grimaced ruefully. Then, 'Do you ever fly the helicopter?'

'Why, are you wishing I was today?' His accompanying glance was chaffing.

She pressed her lips together vexedly but refused to be drawn. 'By that, do I take it you do?'

'Uh-huh,' he owned lazily, but also somewhat vaguely, causing Gayna to realise suddenly that they were slowing and that he had his mind back on the business at hand.

When they came to a halt the second vehicle, with Norm at the wheel and Felicity waving and smiling archly at Ford as they passed, continued on for some distance before stopping ahead and to the left of them. The third vehicle, with an out-of-humour Alwyn aboard, did the same on their right so that they were aligned in a V formation.

'Now we wait,' surmised Gayna with a nervous grin, beginning to feel the first stirrings of restlessness as she anticipated the animals' appearance.

Ford tilted his head skywards, the plane in sight now and skimming the tree-tops. 'But let's hope not for long,' he smiled in return. 'By the look of that, I reckon we should be able to see them any minute now.'

He wasn't wrong, for he had hardly finished speaking before the first grey beast lunged into view, swiftly followed by a great many more, and then all three vehicles were on the move again.

After that the rest of the morning passed in a kaleidoscope of unfamiliar sights and sounds for Gayna as the buffalo were harried into some semblance of a herd by the trucks and driven out on to the plains. In the tail vehicle, it was Ford's job to see that none of them lagged behind, and as this entailed their continual criss-crossing from side to side at the rear of the widely spaced mob, they seemed to be doing the most travelling—as well as collecting the most dust. For a time

Gayna also suspected they were attacting the most cantankerous bulls too!

The first two to decide they'd had enough of being mustered and would rather return to the valley were persuaded otherwise by a chase which had the truck swerving and sliding round trees and termite mounds at breakneck speed before succeeding in heading them back towards the others again—an exercise which had Gayna hanging on to her hat with one hand and the truck with the other, while every high speed change in direction either had her leaning precariously near the open doorway, or else almost toppling into Ford's lap.

The third animal to take exception to their arbitrary treatment, however, was quite another matter. Obviously older, and certainly much larger than the previous two, he clearly considered a frontal attack was the best means of ridding himself of their irritating presence, and lowering his enormous head he charged straight for the front of the vehicle.

The force with which he hit it Gayna felt all the way down to her toes, but she presumed the buffalo must have felt much the same because he promptly went down on his knees. Not that it seemed to deter him at all, because he was up again almost immediately and willingly attempting it once more from a shorter range in a show of strength against the truck which Ford kept edging forward in order to convince him who was the most powerful.

Eventually, the animal must have realised it was losing ground and, in its frustration, turned to hooking its great upward-sweeping horns into its opponent instead. On a number of occasions this proved quite successful as they locked with the bull-bar or else caught beneath the front fenders, whereupon he was able to give the vehicle a jolting shake, but when he seemed to be heading farther and farther around her side, Gayna judiciously decided it was time to move and slid decidedly closer to her companion. The dogs in the back, on their feet now ever since the buffalo had been in sight—although Gayna never knew how they managed to maintain their balance during those furious chases—watched the proceedings with bright intelligent eyes but didn't utter a sound.

Without having taken his eyes from the attacking bull, it was obvious Ford was still aware of Gayna's change in position, and his lips twitched irrepressibly. 'It takes a cranky buffalo to have you voluntarily moving closer to a man, does it, sweetheart?' he taunted.

'Something like that,' she purred facetiously. 'Because if there'd been another choice available, I would have chosen it in preference, believe me!'

'Cat!' he laughed, unperturbed, and yanked her hat down over her eyes.

Gayna removed it altogether, then replaced it in its previous comfortable position. 'I suggest you concentrate on him,' pointing to their attacker as he continued worrying at the truck, 'instead of teasing me,' she counselled, trying to look repressive but failing completely owing to the smile which she couldn't keep off her lips. 'He'll have one of those horns into that tyre if you're not careful, and then what'll we do?'

'Change it,' he drawled in the driest of tones.

Her eyes widened expressively. 'With him around?'

'He won't be for much longer,' grinned Ford with the knowledge of past practice. 'Here comes the chopper now to take him off our hands.'

Gayna craned her neck backwards, shielding her eyes

from the sun with her hand, and acknowledging Brett's wave as he brought the plane in low enough to distract the buffalo's attention and, having done so, allow the truck to resume its patrolling.

As they drove off Gayna swung round to see how he was faring and clapped a hand over her mouth in dismay to see the beast now attempting to catch the helicopter's landing rails with its horns as it hovered only a foot or two or so above him.

'Oh, my God, he's going to bring the plane down!' she couldn't restrain herself from gasping.

Ford didn't even bother to look. 'I doubt it, Brett's too experienced at this sort of work to let that happen.'

'But he's so close to the ground!' she exclaimed, frowning.

'No one ever said aerial mustering wasn't without its dangers,' he shrugged aside her misgivings impassively. 'But you can rest assured Brett knows what he's doing, all the same.'

'I certainly hope so,' she averred, swivelling round again for another look. 'Oh, he's got it moving again, thank heavens!' It was a relieved report she had to make this time as she reverted to looking ahead. A sideways glance at Ford almost immediately followed. 'Do you fly that low too when you pilot the helicopter?' she quizzed.

'If it's necessary,' he owned idly, slowing to allow the now resignedly trotting buffalo to get in front of them so they could take over from Brett, and thereby enable him to return to keeping an eye on the main herd. 'Sometimes, as you just saw, it's the only way you can get the blighters to move.'

'I didn't realise it could be that hazardous,' she mused thoughtfully. 'I suppose at that height it would be all too easy to crash, wouldn't it?'

'Oh, it's not so bad out here in the open, but when you get in among the bush and you need to come down that low, it can get a bit hectic then on occasion.'

An understatement if ever she'd heard one, decided Gayna wryly. She could imagine herself being in a permanent state of panic if faced with such hair-raising experience.

'Have you had your pilot's licence for long?' she asked next.

'About eleven years, fixed-wing, and eight years, rotor,' he supplied with a half laugh. 'Why?'

Because she was unaccountably interested, she abruptly realised, and with no little dismay. Not that she had any intention of telling him that, of course.

'I was just wondering,' she parried. 'You seem to treat it so casually.'

'Mmm, I guess it does become second nature after a time, and especially when you have long distances to cover. Then, it's the only way to travel.' White teeth gleamed in a devastating smile. 'As Alwyn would probably tell you.'

Gayna caught his meaning immediately, and couldn't forbear a grin of her own. 'No, I don't think he was terribly impressed with his journey in the supply truck,' she conceded ruefully. 'Nor with being sent out here today either, actually.'

'I gathered as much from his expression when I saw him getting into the truck.' Pausing for a moment, Ford looked a trifle more contemplative. 'Although I'd have thought knowing you were going along would have cheered him somewhat.'

'I don't see why!' she burst out incredulously.

'Well, according to Snow, Alwyn apparently let it

slip yesterday that he's—er—hoping to persuade you in the very near future into putting your association with him on an—umm—more binding footing?' he revealed, not without some mockery evident.

'Hah! All he wants on a binding footing is the agency! The sly, conniving little pipsqueak!' she decried in disgust. 'As far as I'm concerned, my association with him is just fine as it is . . . distant!'

The arch of his brows peaked sardonically higher. 'I thought you said yesterday you were glad of his interest in your family affairs?'

He would have to remember that! 'You must have misunderstood me,' she evaded, airily nonchalant.

'I might have done in the beginning, but I think I'm on to the right wavelength now,' he returned lazily.

The enigmatic remark had Gayna eyeing him uneasily and prudently opting for another change in subject.

'Is that where you have your yards hidden?' she asked hurriedly, seeing that all three vehicles appeared to be driving the herd towards a large patch of scrub in front of them.

'That's right,' he corroborated, easing his foot down on the accelerator. The buffalo, thinking it their chance to escape, were breaking into a gallop again in their desire to reach the covering trees as soon as possible. 'And this is also where we have to watch that none of them get away on us.'

'Will they return to the valley if they do?'

'Perhaps not immediately, but it wouldn't be long before they found their way back again.'

The flank vehicles were closing in on the animals now, forcing them nearer together and imperceptibly guiding them towards the long, funnel-shaped opening

to the trap. The first of the buffalo entered unsuspect-
ingly enough, until they came in sight of the solid steel
yards awaiting at the end, whereupon they promptly
tried to turn back on their fellows.

For a time pandemonium reigned as the snorting
beasts jostled each other and kicked up clouds of veil-
ing dust. The dogs, set working now, barked and
chivvied at them till they were facing in the right
direction once more, while the helicopter and three
escorting vehicles ensured that none of the milling animals at the rear managed to elude them in the mêlée.

At last order was restored and the trucks closed ranks
behind the buffalo, following them down to the yards,
and keeping them packed so tightly together that it
was impossible for them to move in any direction
except forward. The men who had driven out earlier
to make ready for them were working the gates on the
yards—separating those that were to be retained from
those to be shipped away—and because of the animals'
unwillingness to be penned at all, the process was a
slow and lengthy one. Finally, however, the nine-foot-
high entrance gate was clanged shut behind the tail-
enders and everyone could relax.

'How many were there altogether, do you know?'
Gayna asked of Ford as he reversed the truck before
driving it around to where the others had parked in
some shade.

'About sixty, I'd reckon,' he estimated, then called
to the aboriginal stockman who had been operating the
first gate, 'What was the tally, Jake?'

'Sixty-five, boss,' came the readily grinned reply.
'Not a bad morning's haul, eh?'

'Not bad at all,' Ford affirmed with an answering
smile as they drove off.

Gayna turned to him queryingly. 'Now what?'

'Well, I don't know about you, but I'm heading for the bore trough to wash some of this dust off,' he drawled wryly.

'I'll be in that,' she approved devoutly, wiping beads of perspiration from her forehead with the back of one hand. 'Of course, it will be a case of ladies first, I trust,' she added facetiously.

'The trough's nearly thirty feet long, sweetheart,' he advised lazily, mockingly. 'I think you'll find there's room enough for us to share.'

In actual fact, Gayna wouldn't have minded sharing if it had been only three feet long. She felt as if she had been breathing nothing but fine red dust for a week, and her only concern at that moment was to rid herself of it as quickly as possible!

CHAPTER EIGHT

LUNCH consisted of specially prepared buffalo steaks and vegetables cooked over an open fire, but because Alwyn didn't really know anyone else there and had obtrusively seated himself some distance apart in any case, Gayna reluctantly felt obliged to keep him company.

'What do you think of the buffalo meat?' she asked conversationally as she joined him.

His mouth promptly turned down disdainfully in what she suddenly realised was an almost habitual gesture. 'Revolting!' he slated explicitly. 'The same as this whole morning's operation has been.'

'I found it rather interesting, actually,' she persevered as best she was able. In truth, she felt it would have been no more than he deserved if she'd left him on his own. 'As for the meat—well, I admit it certainly does have a different taste from beef, but not one that I would really have called unpleasant. Just stronger flavoured.'

'Hmm.' Disgruntled, he deliberately pushed the meat to one side of his plate and began picking fastidiously at the vegetables heaped thereon. 'Maybe it would have tasted better if I could have washed before eating, but they wouldn't let me use the water they'd brought with them,' he now complained.

'The bore trough was good enough for everyone else,' she pointed out a little tersely. Even Felicity, she'd noted, who was now busily intent on engaging Ford's attention.

His expression became one of scornful hauteur. 'Well, I certainly had no intention of washing in water those filthy great beasts have been drinking from, I can assure you!'

'No one expected you to,' she advised drily. 'If you'd bothered to look, you would have discovered that we washed in the water *before* it reached the pens. Not vice versa.'

'Oh!' Briefly, he looked discomfited. 'Then why didn't anyone tell me that?'

'They probably didn't get a chance amid your demands to use the drinking water,' she proposed eloquently.

Alwyn grimaced sourly but didn't immediately reply. Then, when he did, it was to change the subject and in a completely different tone of voice from the querulous one he had been using. 'Look, about last night . . .' he began coaxingly.

'I'd rather not talk about it, if you don't mind,' Gayna cut him off peremptorily.

'Yes, well, I'm sorry if—if you thought I was going too fast for you, but we still have this matter with Therese to discuss, you know,' he came back hastily, if a little selfconsciously at the start.

'Do we?' She eyed him cynically. 'I happen to disagree. As I told you yesterday, I think it's a lost cause, anyway, but as I also had it succinctly pointed out to me this morning, that not once has Mum *asked* for either of our opinions, then I'm afraid I think the time has come for us to keep our thoughts to ourselves and to accept her decision with as much grace as possible.'

'That's all right for you to say, she'll no doubt make sure you don't lose by it, but what about me?' he exclaimed on a resentful note.

'Well, what about you?' she couldn't help countering angrily. 'As yet there's been no mention at all of her selling the agency, but should there be in future then I'm just as positive, knowing Mum, that she'll stand by any agreement she's made!'

'Provided her new husband agrees, of course!' he jeered.

'Lachlan's already explained it's entirely up to Mum what she does with the business!'

'Oh, yes, naturally he'd say something like that before they were married! Afterwards, it's likely to be a totally different story, though, isn't it?'

'Is it?' Her winged brows arched expressively. 'I would have thought the Montgomerys had plenty of businesses of their own to occupy their time without worrying about the agency.'

'Then you've changed your mind considerably since we discussed the matter in Adelaide!' he charged.

'Perhaps I've had reason to!'

'I can't imagine what it was,' he sneered, looking directly towards Ford.

Gayna's eyes sparked wrathfully. 'Oh, don't be such a fool!' she castigated. 'I was meaning, by what I'd learnt about Lachlan!'

'From Therese?' sardonically.

'Plus my own observations! And he isn't the type to dissemble.'

'How about the son and heir?'

'Ford? What's it to do with him?'

'Well, at dinner last night he certainly sounded to me as if he had more than his share to say in the running of the place.'

'With regard to Mundamunda, I think he has—as well as their other ventures, for all I'm aware,' she conceded, shrugging. 'But he wouldn't have where Mum's investments are concerned, I'm sure.'

'I'm not,' Alwyn disagreed trenchantly. 'I wouldn't put it past that arbitrary swine to persuade her into selling just out of pure vindictiveness because I had the audacity to come up here uninvited!'

Gayna shook her head in disbelief. 'Now you really are being ridiculous!' she accused derisively. 'Besides which, I'm sorry to have to puncture your vanity, but I sincerely doubt if Ford considers you of sufficient significance to warrant any vengefulness on his part.'

'You expect me to believe that?' Alwyn patently didn't!

'Quite frankly, I couldn't care less whether you do or not,' she informed him in bittersweet tones as she rose to her feet. 'Because not only do you over-estimate your importance, but you also overrate my patience with your continual self-preoccupation and your peevish gripings!'

'I didn't ask you to join me!' he retaliated, his thin lips curling into a sneer.

'Thank you for reminding me. I shall endeavour not to make the same mistake again!' she smiled acidly, and departed with eager haste.

Shortly after they had finished eating the cattle trucks arrived—all bearing the name *Montgomery Transport* on their doors, Gayna observed wryly—and the laborious job of loading the unco-operative buffalo began. It was hot and dusty work beneath the blazing sun and before long all the men had shed their shirts as perspiration trickled down sinewed, mahogany backs due to their exertions in prodding, urging, and physically pressuring the beasts into doing as they wished.

It was dangerous work too for the buffalo thought nothing of charging into the square steel rails, or of sweeping their long horns between those rails in an effort to catch the unwary, and many was the time that Gayna's heart leapt into her mouth to see someone escape by only a few inches from being impaled on those ridged points.

Deeming it the most judicious for all concerned, she kept well out of the men's way by watching from a not too uncomfortable position in the shade and atop one of the mustering vehicle's bonnets, while Alwyn displayed his uninterest by sitting against a tree with his back to the whole scene and furiously swatting at the numerous flies present.

Felicity, on the other hand, was only too anxious to show her interest in the proceedings by flitting from one place to the other—first by the loading ramp, and then by the pens—and nearly always getting in somebody's road until, after she almost collided with Brett one time, he told her in no uncertain terms to, 'Get the hell out of the way!'

Although she looked to Ford to countermand the order, on finding him with his attention engrossed elsewhere, Felicity had no choice but to accede, which she did with a haughty sniff as she flounced towards the truck beside Gayna's.

'One of these days it will give me the greatest of pleasure to put Brett Daniels in *his* place for a change!' she muttered direfully, but obviously for Gayna's edification.

Since she couldn't pretend not to have heard what either of them said, Gayna tried a peace-keeping role. 'He was probably distracted, but I expect it was only your welfare he was thinking about,' she excused.

'Hah! Brett Danials just likes to throw his weight around!' came the amending retort. 'And I, for one, won't be at all sorry to see the last of him when he leaves to take up his own property.'

'He and Raeleen are leaving Mundamunda?' Gayna queried in surprise.

'Mmm, in a couple of months. They've just bought a place up on the Cape,' Felicity disclosed negligently. A malicious little smile began playing about her mouth. 'Then, when Snow and your mother leave as well, Ford and I will be able to make Mundamunda *our* home. Cosy, hmm?'

'Very,' agreed Gayna stiffly, wondering why she should find it such a troubling possibility. However, the blonde had made another disturbing revelation too, and she hurried on to question with a frown, 'But what do you mean, when Lachlan and Mum leave as well?'

'Don't you know? Well, maybe no one's mentioned it to Therese yet either,' Felicity partly laughed, partly smirked. 'Nonetheless, Ford has confided in *me*,' with triumphant emphasis, 'that Snow is very keen to take a closer interest in Baapanannia once it goes into production.'

'To the extent of leaving Mundamunda permanently?' Gayna persisted, unable to quite believe it.

'Well, of course! If—when,' Felicity corrected herself hastily, 'Ford and I marry, naturally we won't want to be sharing our home with another couple . . . even if one of them does happen to be his father.'

That tell-tale slip of the tongue allowed Gayna to breathe easier. Felicity was nowhere near as certain of her ground as she claimed to be. Now, schooling her features into a picture of innocence, she allowed,

'No, of course not. It's just that I didn't realise mat-

ters had—er—progressed so far between yourself and
Ford. I can see I shall have to offer him my con-
gratulations.'

'Don't you dare!' forbade Felicity, reddening to her
hairline. 'It's nothing to do with you! Besides, it—it's
a secret still. Ford doesn't want it made public yet in
case it—it detracts from Therese and Snow's wedding,'
she concluded on a frantic gasp.

'Oh, I see,' Gayna nodded, trying not to smile, pityingly. Judging by Felicity's abrupt volte-face, she was
no nearer to capturing Ford than she had ever been.
'Well, I must say it's very generous of you to have
taken me into your confidence.'

'As long as that's how it stays . . . a confidence,' the
other girl threatened. 'I don't want all and sundry
knowing my plans!'

And especially not Ford, Gayna was willing to bet.
Aloud, she promised melodramatically, 'Rest assured,
my lips are sealed!'

An avowal which, perhaps not surprisingly, had
Felicity looking at her suspiciously askance, before
she returned her attention to what was happening in
the yards. Gayna's interest therein wasn't quite as
absorbed now, though, as at least one particular aspect
of her conversation with the older girl stayed in the
forefront of her mind. Was Lachlan intending to leave
Mundamunda in the not too distant future, and if so,
was her mother aware of the fact? Or had that just
been another figment of Felicity's overworked imagination, like the rest of her wishful thinking? she
pondered.

Soon, the engine of the truck taking the selected
calves back to the homestead rent the air, and began
rolling away from its loading ramp in an inevitable haze

of red dust. The second, a double-decker road train containing the bulk of the herd, wasn't long in following, and as soon as the two vehicles were on their way across the plains the job of cleaning up and packing gear started.

Then, after the men had partaken of another head-submerging, dust-removing wash, the helicopter and the mustering vehicles left one by one—Alwyn, with as much harrying and hurrying as ever the dogs had done, making certain his was the first to depart—until only Ford's truck remained. A cursory inspection of the site was all that was needed to satisfy himself everything had been left as it should be, and then he was calling the dogs out from beneath the vehicle where they had been enjoying a well-earned, tongue-lolling rest and, taking his own seat at the wheel, ordered them up behind him—just as Gayna was preparing to resumed her place.

Probably because they were unused to passengers being carried in the truck, the dogs immediately bounced between her legs, on to the seat, and over the back in order to take up their customary positions, but in the process caused Gayna to trip and had her doing what she had managed to avoid all morning . . . falling squarely into Ford's lap.

'I'm sorry,' she mumbled, flushing, and acutely embarrassed to find her hands in contact with a bare, muscled thigh as she rushed to push herself away from him.

Ford's hands clasped her shoulders in a steadying grip, but made no effort to help her in putting more distance between them. 'That's okay, it wasn't your fault. Besides . . .' the curve of his sensuous mouth swept upwards in a captivating grin, 'I've never objected to attractive young females throwing themselves at me,' he drawled.

Flustered beyond belief, Gayna just couldn't hold his teasing blue gaze and she concentrated her vision on the expanse of tanned chest visible between the gaping edges of his half buttoned shirt.

'I w-wasn't throwing myself at y-you,' she faltered breathlessly.

'No, you'd rather take two steps backward than one forward where a man was involved, wouldn't you, sweetheart?' he bent his dark head to taunt softly.

He was so close she could feel his breath warm against her stained cheek, and she licked at strangely dry lips nervously. She felt as if whatever willpower she did possess was slowly but surely being drained from her, and it was more than she could do to both prevent it from leaving, as well as trade words with him simultaneously.

'It takes all kinds.' She had hoped to sound defiant, but it was too shaky for that, she realised in despair.

'But not manufactured ones at variance with their true characters,' he disputed huskily, turning her face up to his.

Knowing he intended kissing her, Gayna fought against his hold in panic. 'No! Please!' she first ordered and then entreated as his mouth descended.

Not to be denied, Ford ignored both as he inexorably took possession of her soft lips, and quelled her desperate struggles with an almost insolent ease. A maelstrom of differing emotions exploded within Gayna in response—anger, resentment, dismay, apprehension, but perhaps strongest and most disturbing of all, she was conscious of a quickening within her that was ruthlessly sapping her resistance, and replacing it with an electrifying sensation that racked her entire being.

Pliantly, she allowed muscular arms to enfold her, her lips moving invitingly beneath his as they willingly submitted to his burning demands, her hands involuntarily seeking contact with the taut flesh of his chest. For Gayna, it was a new and somewhat bewildering experience, one which made her feel both exhilarated and vulnerable at the same time, but one she also knew she was powerless to control.

Sensing her capitulation, Ford began a fresh assault on her emotions as his mouth traced fiery exploratory paths to her eyes, her ears, the sensitive areas of her arching throat, and back to her impatiently waiting lips again. His hands freed her shirt from her jeans, sliding under the thin material to caress the sweep of her alabaster-smooth back with slow, intoxicating movements, and sending a quiver of unfamiliar awareness coursing through her when he deftly unfastened her shirt and then as efficiently disposed of the clasp on her bra.

With his hand cupping one full, swelling breast, his thumb gently brushing across the already thrusting, throbbing nipple, Gayna trembled convulsively as her body wantonly thrilled to every stimulating touch—a wantonness that merged with an unparalleled desire when his questing lips tantalisingly took the place of his arousing thumb.

'Dear God, you're the most glorious creature I've ever laid eyes on!' Ford groaned in a deep voice, heavy with emotion, against the creamy mound of her breast.

Gayna's eyelids fluttered open to reveal slumbrous green eyes with a hint of confusion in their depths. It had all happened with such breathtaking swiftness, she didn't know what to say. She wasn't even quite sure how it had managed to advance to such an uninhibited stage. At the moment her only knowledge seemed to be centred on his devastating ability to breach her defences as no one ever had before.

'Oh, please, let me go!' she begged helplessly at length, and trying to shield her mortifying nakedness from him now.

'Perhaps I'd better,' he acceded in a none too even tone, his mouth tilting crookedly as he brushed her tousled hair away from her face with a gentle hand. 'Because unless I miss my guess, there's a vehicle heading in this direction.'

Gayna could hear its rumbling approach herself now, and with a gasp of dismay she hurriedly re-clipped her bra back into place. The buttons on her shirt proved another matter, however, for in her haste her fingers fumbled and in the end, with a lazy smile for her predicament, it was Ford who attended to them for her— a circumstance which did nothing to lessen her self-consciousness, and especially not since the vehicle, with Felicity and Norm aboard, arrived before she could push her shirt back into her jeans.

'*He* wasn't overly enthusiastic at the idea,' Felicity indicated the wryly expressioned stockman beside her with a grimace, 'but when I couldn't see you following us, I insisted we return in case something had happened,' she explained.

'No, nothing's happened,' Ford denied blandly. 'We were just about to leave when we heard you coming.'

'Then what kept you so long?'

'I wasn't aware we had been. It didn't seem long to me,' he drawled so evocatively that Gayna couldn't control the rush of colour that flooded into her cheeks.

'Oh?' Felicity's eyes glittered coldly as they noted the younger girl's reaction. 'Well, poor Gayna doesn't look as if she would agree with you. In fact, I'd say she looks most discomfited,' she laughed maliciously. Returning her attention to Ford, she became coy. 'If you've been teasing her again about that brilliantly red hair of hers, perhaps it would be an idea if she and I changed places on the way home.'

Gayna needed no second bidding and, scooping her hat up from the floor where it had fallen, was out of the truck as soon as Felicity had finished speaking. Now that her head was back in charge she could think more clearly, and she didn't intend Ford to complacently believe she was just another of his casual conquests. Twice now he might have broken through her defences, but that didn't mean she was willing to be a member of the team for the type of game he obviously liked to play. As far as she was concerned, Felicity and all his other admirers were welcome to him!

'I'm agreeable,' she answered with an indifferent shrug as she made for the other vehicle. 'I expect you and Ford have a lot to talk about, anyway.' She left everyone to specify exactly what in their own minds.

Both Felicity's and Norm's faces cheered significantly, although what Ford's thoughts were on the matter Gayna had no idea. She deliberately kept her back to him so she couldn't find out. Either way, unconcerned or otherwise, she wasn't sure she really wanted to know.

'Your shirt's out,' Felicity remarked, eyes narrowing mistrustfully, as they passed.

Gayna had no trouble in parrying such comments now that she was free from Ford's imbalancing presence. 'It's cooler this way,' she asserted calmly, and climbed up beside Norm.

The return to the homestead was accomplished speedily, and without anything else exceptional occurring, but today it was Gayna who went searching for her mother immediately on arrival. She found her tucked away in a leafy arbour shaded by a magnificent rust-coloured bougainvillea in the garden, busily attending to some business papers.

Therese's expression became guarded as she watched her daughter sink on to a chair beside her, and seeing it Gayna sighed sadly. She couldn't remember them even having been this estranged before.

'I owe you an apology, don't I?' she began slowly, contritely. 'I've been behaving as if you need my consent to get married, and I'm sorry. It's your decision to make, not mine.'

Momentarily, her mother's features relaxed, then promptly firmed again as she questioned watchfully, 'Does that mean you believe your opposition to have been unfounded, or that it will just be unvoiced from now on?'

'Unfounded, I guess,' Gayna made herself smile ruefully. It was so clearly what her mother wanted to hear that she hadn't the heart to disappoint her any more by trying to explain that the reasons for her opposition—unvoiced though they would now be—were still unchanged.

'Oh, darling, you've no idea how relieved you've made me!' Therese caught hold of Gayna's hand ecstatically. 'All I ever wanted was for you to wish us happiness.'

'But I've never wished either of you anything else,' Gayna felt obliged to point out, if somewhat wryly. 'I just tried to ensure it in a more—umm—cautious manner, that's all.'

Therese smiled indulgently, all her worries gone now. 'And Lachlan will be pleased too, I know,' she ran on happily. 'You do like him, don't you, Gayna?'

This was easier ground, allowing her to reply more truthfully. 'Yes, I do, very much as a matter of fact,' she owned. 'He seems very kind and considerate.'

'And Ford and Raeleen?'

Gayna suspected her mother was attempting to play Happy Families, and for her sake she made an effort to go along with it. 'If I have to have a stepbrother and sister, I guess they'll do,' she joked lightly. Not that she minded Raeleen, of course, and as she anticipated seeing either of them only rarely, what was to be gained by saying anything else?

'I'm so pleased,' Therese sighed elatedly. 'Now I know there'll be nothing to stop you from spending all your holidays with us, because I don't intend to lose contact with my only natural daughter, you know.'

Spend all her holidays with them . . . and Ford? Gayna couldn't think of anything worse! 'Yes— well . . .' she stammered, her brain racing for an excuse, and chancing on that remark of Felicity's. 'Anyway, I understand you might be moving soon . . . to Baapanannia. Is that right?'

'Well, yes, Lachlan and I have discussed it,' Therese owned, frowning slightly. 'Although even if we do, I'm not quite sure what difference that makes to your spending your holidays with us.'

All the difference in the world, to Gayna's way of thinking. It meant Ford would be at Mundamunda!

'It doesn't really, I suppose,' she was now willing to concede. 'I just thought that . . .' Deliberately leaving her explanation unfinished, she mentioned instead, 'Raeleen and Brett will be moving soon too, I hear.'

'Mmm, that's right. It's beginning to look as if Ford will be the only one left at Mundamunda very shortly,' came the laughing reply.

Uncertain as to why she should be interested, Gayna still had to ask, 'And he'll be marrying Felicity, I presume?'

'Good grief, why on earth would you presume that?'

Gayna found the astonishment in her mother's voice strangely soothing. 'Well, she's always with him, and—and . . .'

'And it's going to take someone with a lot more than Felicity's got to have Ford heading up the aisle, you mark my words!' Therese cut in drily.

'Mmm, he's very like my father in many ways, isn't he?' Gayna grimaced tartly.

'Lord, no!' Therese found the comparison so unlikely that she laughed. 'You couldn't find anyone *less* like him if you tried.'

'But—but you just said he'd want more than Felicity had to offer, and my father was always open to what he thought might be a better deal, wasn't he?' Gayna puzzled.

'Except that where Felicity is concerned, I meant she needed more . . . personality-wise,' advised Therese wryly.

'Oh!' Gayna hunched one slim shoulder disconcertedly. 'Well, he's still like him in the way he enjoys having women make fools of themselves over him,' she insisted obdurately.

'Oh?' It was Therese's turn to remark, one eyebrow peaking ironically. 'And just what, might I ask, makes you so knowledgeable regarding his likes and dislikes concerning women?'

Gayna was only too pleased to tell her. 'Because he

makes it so obvious!' she disparaged scornfully. 'I mean, you've just said you don't think he'll marry Felicity, yet I haven't exactly seen him trying to fend her off when she clutches hold of him with such nauseating regularity! Nor was he trying to evade the girl I saw him with at the airport in Darwin. She was clinging to him like a lovesick idiot too!' Taking a deep breath, she concluded witheringly, 'He encourages them, in fact!'

Therese's lips twitched with amusement. 'Darling, of course women are going to throw themselves at him, he's an extremely good-looking man. However, you can't blame him for that, and really, I think you're mistaking mere politeness on his part for something else entirely.'

Was she? It certainly hadn't been out of politeness that he'd made love to her this afternoon. No, that had been because—like all attractive men—he couldn't stand the thought of any female remaining immune to his so-called charms!

'Politeness?' she scoffed. 'More like, vanity, you mean!'

'Oh, Gayna,' her mother murmured disappointedly. 'You're not going to let this thing you have about your father rub off on to Ford, just because he happens to be the epitome of "tall, dark, and handsome", are you?'

Suspecting she had already revealed too much, Gayna put a brake on her feelings, her mobile mouth shaping ruefully. 'Sorry, I have been going on at length, haven't I? Shall we talk about something else?'

Therese accepted with alacrity. 'We could think of some more things for you to see and do while you're here, if you like,' she suggested.

'Yes—well—that was something I wanted to discuss with you too,' Gayna smiled faintly, combing her fingers through her hair and shifting uncomfortably on her seat. 'Since the reason for my visit was supposed to be, ostensibly, to satisfy myself you weren't—er—being conned into this marriage, I thought now that's been settled, I'd like to go home with Alwyn tomorrow, if that's all right by you.'

'You want to go back *with* Alwyn?' Therese's tone was incredulous.

'Well, not exactly with him, just at the same time,' Gayna clarified diffidently.

'But why? I thought now that the air had been cleared between us, we might be able to find some things to do together.'

'I'd like that, of course, but . . .'

'You'd rather get back to the city?' Therese guessed.

Gayna grabbed at the excuse offered with both hands. 'You know I've never really been a fan for the outback,' she laughed weakly.

'You enjoyed yourself yesterday and today, though, didn't you?'

Enjoyed having her well-ordered existence thrown into chaos by a man she hardly knew? That was the very reason she wanted to leave!

'Both days were certainly enlightening,' was all she would admit.

Therese leant forward persuasively. 'I was hoping you'd at least stay until I leave in a fortnight's time. Then we could go back together.'

While spending another two weeks wondering whether her self-control would disconcertingly vanish as disastrously as it had this afternoon if confronted by Ford's overwhelming masculinity again?

'No, I don't think I'd better,' she smiled apologetically, not wanting to hurt her mother's feelings. 'It was never my intention to stay longer than a week, in any case, and . . .' she spread her hands meaningfully, 'well, you know yourself, we are short-handed at the agency at the moment. I think it would be fairer if I did return. After all, I suppose I shall have to take time off again shortly, for the wedding.' Her brows lifted enquiringly. 'I gather you'll be married up here in the Territory?'

'Mmm, we thought in Darwin, as a matter of fact,' Therese confirmed meditatively. Then, with her sherry brown eyes wryly intent, 'You do realise, of course, that if you go back with Alwyn tomorrow afternoon, you'll have to stay overnight in town because there's not another plane going south until early the following morning, don't you?'

The flight timetable was the least of Gayna's worries. 'It can't be helped, I guess,' she shrugged unconcernedly. Even an evening spent in Alwyn's less than exhilarating company would be preferable to the emotional catastrophe she had experienced at Mundamunda today!

'Well, if you're determined to go . . .' Therese sighed in resignation. 'I'll let Ford know he has another passenger when I see him next.'

'Thank you,' Gayna acknowledged, relieved. After Ford's previous insistence that she wouldn't be leaving with Alwyn, she hadn't been looking forward to informing him that she intended flouting his wishes after all.

She was still half expecting some opposition to her decision from Ford, nevertheless—or at least an accusation that she was running away again—when they all

adjourned to the lounge later that night for coffee and
Therese brought up the matter of her return to
Adelaide. But when no such contradiction was voiced,
she was uncertain as to whether she felt relieved or
bereaved by his lack of interest.

'But you've really only just arrived!' exclaimed
Raeleen with a frown as everyone, except Ford, expressed their surprise on hearing of her resolve.

'Yes, I know,' Gayna smiled deprecatingly. 'But
since I can see how right Mum and Lachlan are together,' it was funny how the more often she said that,
the more she came to think it the truth, 'and as the
agency is short-staffed at present, I thought it would
be best all round if I returned as soon as possible.'

'As well as that, don't forget, Gayna isn't a lover of
the country life, as we all are,' put in Felicity helpfully.
If it hastened the younger girl on her way, she was
obviously all for it.

'Well, whatever the reason, it's Gayna's decision to
make,' Lachlan inserted with kindly protectiveness.
'As long as she remembers she's welcome at
Mundamunda any time she cares to visit.' And after
returning Gayna's grateful smile with an understanding one of his own, he focussed his gaze on his son as
he surmised, 'You'll be flying Gayna and Alwyn to
Darwin tomorrow, I take it?'

Ford shook his head in negation. 'No, I won't,
actually,' he advised in the coolest of disinterested
tones. 'I've arranged to go over to Oroya Park tomorrow,' naming a neighbouring property.

Two perplexed furrows made an appearance above
Gayna's daintily shaped nose. That was curious, she
mused. She was sure he'd intended flying Alwyn to
Darwin when he was to be the only passenger. Or was

this, perhaps, just his way of stopping her from leaving?

'I'll take the chopper when I go, though, and that'll leave the other free for Brett to fly them to Darwin,' Ford unconsciously dashed her theory—or was it hopes?—to pieces when he started speaking again. 'He won't mind standing in for me, I'm sure,' he grinned lazily—and for the first time that evening, Gayna realised—but at his brother-in-law.

'No, I don't mind,' Brett concurred readily. 'A nice easy flight like . . .'

'And I'll go with *you*,' Felicity chopped him off in her eagerness to invite herself along with Ford. 'It's ages since I've seen Megan Abercrombie.' She cast him a coquettish glance. 'You won't object to me accompany you, will you?'

'No, you're welcome to join me if you want, honey,' he granted with indulgent good humour, and whether he was aware of it or not, had Gayna glowering at him contemptuously.

The nagging ache in the region of her chest that had assailed her on hearing his ready acceptance of Felicity's company on the morrow, she resolutely ignored. He reminded her of a bee, she charged silently, sarcastically, only he took what he wanted from every female who came his way, but just like a bee he owned allegiance to none! Today, herself; tomorrow, Felicity; the day after . . . Megan Abercrombie, perhaps?

Her throat constricted as she remembered the way in which she had adolescently succumbed to his caresses, and temporarily, her eyes closed in despair. When they opened again they were bright with renewed determination. Well, at least she could console herself with the knowledge that he wasn't likely to have the opportunity to make such a fool of her again!

At the same time, however, and much to her irritation, she did still find herself wondering if such assuredness was only possible due to her less than heroic decision to beat a rapid retreat!

CHAPTER NINE

FROM the moment she arrived back in Adelaide, Gayna filled every minute of her time with work, and more work in an effort to keep her thoughts from straying to memories she was all too anxious to forget. To her annoyance and frustration, Ford's lazily drawling voice was proving extremely difficult to dispel from her ears, his lithe image even more impossible to eject from her mind.

Most evenings she put off going to bed until long after twelve, because she knew without a doubt that sleep would mockingly elude her for hours, or when it did eventually overtake her, it would be laden with dreams of warm, demanding lips and knowing, caressing hands, from which she would awaken in a lather of perspiration and consumed by an unknown longing.

It didn't seem to make any difference that she kept telling herself he wasn't worth remembering; her brain appeared determined to think otherwise. The suspicion that she might have unconsciously allowed him to come to mean more to her than he should tormented her on occasion, but she steadfastly refused to believe such an improbability could have occurred. She was the one who was wise to the wiles of men, wasn't she? How could she, of all people, possibly have fallen for one of the slickest she had ever met? No, it wasn't possible, she would deny categorically, agonisingly. She just couldn't be in love with Ford Montgomery . . . could she?

By the second week after her return even Alwyn began to comment that she was trying to do too much and, although she protested against it, he insisted that she leave early the day before her mother was due home. His reasoning was so that she might ensure everything at the apartment was in readiness for Therese, but housework had been another method she'd used to keep busy and she knew their living quarters were already as clean and polished as they could be.

So, after Alwyn had adamantly ushered her out through the doors of the agency in person, rather than go home immediately to an empty apartment where she would only brood, she went shopping instead. It would, she hoped, give her something else to think about. Not that it turned out to be a very successful ploy, however, for as soon as she entered the supermarket she came face to face with a display advertising the fruits and produce of the tropical north which instantly reminded her of all she was attempting to forget. Feeling her eyes misting traitorously, Gayna about-turned and headed straight for the car park without making a single purchase.

Half an hour or so later she arrived home with her luxuriant lashes still damp, and after garaging her car she dashed the back of her hand furiously across her eyes lest any of their neighbours should be about and see the traces of her foolish reaction to a mere advertisement.

A swift check of the mailbox revealed no letters and she hurried into the building, but as she opened the door to their apartment a cloud of warm air greeted her and she entered with a perplexed frown creasing her forehead.

An expression which was swiftly replaced by one of

incredulity as she saw Ford calmly seated before the fire. Dressed in navy coloured hip-hugging pants with a heavy-knit rollnecked sweater of sky blue that contrasted startlingly with his tanned skin, he looked so flagrantly vital that her chin promptly angled higher in challenge as all her old feelings of animosity came racing back.

'What are you doing here, and how did you get in?' she demanded fiercely. Then, as a thought occurred, 'Did Mum come with you?' And as another quickly followed, 'Has something happened to her?'

'Welcome to you too, sweetheart,' he drily took her to task for her lack of greeting as he rose leisurely to his feet. 'And the answer to your last two questions is, no. As to the other, I opened the door with a key to get in,' bringing forth the proof from his pocket and waving it aggravatingly in front of her. 'Therese gave it to me.'

'That was generous of her,' Gayna snapped, wishing she could say a few words to her mother. Unbuttoning her coat, she tossed both it and her bag on to a printed linen-covered sofa. 'But you still haven't said *why* you're here yet.'

'I'll get round to it . . . when I'm ready,' he drawled in the same lazy tone she had imagined hearing for the past two weeks.

'Suit yourself,' she shrugged repressively, and began making for the kitchen. As she passed him she looked pointedly at the cup of coffee resting on the table beside the chair he'd been using. 'I see you've already made yourself at home, so you won't mind if I make myself a cup, I trust.' Her eyes widened sarcastically.

'Be my guest,' he taunted, waving her on with an exaggerated bow.

Gayna stormed over to the percolator with her breasts heaving resentfully beneath the severely styled blouse she was wearing. Even if her mother had given him a key, how dared he act as if he owned the place! she fumed. Retrieving a cup and saucer from a cupboard above the cinnamon-tiled bench, she set them down with a clatter and, in her anger, somewhat sloppily poured herself some of the still hot liquid.

'What are we having for dinner?' came Ford's goading enquiry from where he leant negligently against the door jamb, watching her.

Gayna added sugar and cream to her cup before answering. She needed the time to control her seething temper!

'I don't know about you, but I was planning to have some diet biscuits,' she lied. Carrying her cup towards him, she flicked her eyes up to his mockingly. 'Care to join me?'

In return, his gaze roamed over her in a measuring survey that missed nothing. 'Is that why you look so pale and washed out? Because you're not eating properly?' he countered.

Little did he know! But since she had no intention of telling him the reason, she just quipped sardonically, 'Thanks for the compliments!' and went to squeeze through the doorway.

Without him moving, however, this proved impossible to accomplish and, with a wrathfully indrawn breath, she glared upwards. 'Are you going to get out of the way, or aren't you?' she smouldered.

'Seeing how you asked so nicely . . . no, I'm not!' he refused with a caustic inflection.

'Be damned to you, then!' she flared, and returned to the bench.

'And be damned to you too, you exasperating little virago, because I've taken just about all I intend to take from you!' Now he moved, relentlessly, towards her.

'You've taken all *you're* going to take!' Gayna emphasised incredulously, but seeing the taut set of his features prudently left her cup where it was and began edging around the kitchen table. 'Well, isn't that too bad! If you don't like it, you can always leave, you know. The door's that way.' She flung out a hand towards the front of the apartment.

Ford merely eyed her backward progress derisively. 'Still running away, hmm?'

'So why should you care?' she challenged, but watching his every move closely. He hadn't stopped following her. 'It didn't seem to worry you when you had Felicity all too willing to chase after you!' She could have bitten her tongue out for having as good as admitted she'd left Mundamunda because of him.

Apparently he thought she had as well, because he suddenly laughed—a reaction which only outraged Gayna's already turbulent feelings further—and drawled sardonically, 'At least Felicity isn't afraid of life.'

'Then go and stalk her round her kitchen table! She'd probably enjoy it . . . I don't!'

'Too scared of your own responses when a man touches you, huh?'

The taunt cut too close to the bone, at least when he was involved. 'No!' she denied vehemently, and as much for her own peace of mind as to convince him. 'I just wish you'd go away and leave me alone, that's all!'

'So you can remain cocooned from the real world?'

'If that means from types like you, then yes, that's

what I want!' she blazed. 'You think all women are yours just for the taking . . . well, we're not! So why don't you go and play your cruel little games with someone else, because I didn't invite you here, and nor do I want you here!' Reaching the corner of the table nearest the doorway, she whirled and headed through the opening, making for her bedroom. At least that door had a lock on it for which he didn't have a key!

Unfortunately, though, she slammed the bedroom door closed behind her with such force that the key which was already in the lock bounced out and fell to the floor, and before she could pick it up the door was opened again and Ford followed her into the room.

'Get out! How dare you come in here!' she exploded furiously, even as she once again was forced to fall back under his steady advance. Then, feeling herself being cornered, she half commanded, half entreated, 'Don't you lay a hand on me, Ford! Just go away and leave me alone!'

'I'll lay a hand on you all I want!' he bit out in a roughening voice and, as if to prove his point, he pinioned her arms behind her back as his mouth clamped down on hers in such a branding kiss of possession that her breath momentarily fled from her body.

Gayna twisted her head free in panic. 'No! I hate you!' she vowed, wrestling helplessly against his grasp.

'Then we'll just have to convert your hate into some other emotion, won't we?' he proposed huskily.

All too aware that he was capable of doing exactly that, she renewed her struggles frantically, a cry of alarm escaping her when he tumbled them both on to the bed.

'Ford, no! Please don't make . . .'

The rest of her plea was lost as his lips closed over hers again, and seconds later Gayna knew she was lost too. As he had implied, it was herself she'd been fighting all along, not him, she realised, and his drugging kisses were robbing her of the will to continue as they elicited a response she found impossible to control.

On a partly sobbed, partly moaned sigh, her lips parted softly, willingly, her body moulding itself to the muscular outline of his rugged frame, her hands, freed now, finding their way beneath his sweater to savour the firm, rippling flesh of his back.

Ford shuddered expressively and drew her even nearer, his deep, vibrant voice murmuring words she couldn't distinguish against her increasingly feverish skin, his fingers wandering exploringly from one enticing curve to the next as if attempting to memorise her lissome form by touch.

When he eventually raised his head, it was to scan her flushed features with ebony-framed eyes still warm with desire. 'You were made for love, sweetheart, not hate,' he groaned on a tense, uneven note.

Gayna turned her head away sharply, tears welling into her eyes for the second time that afternoon, but only to have it quickly swung back again by a forceful hand spanning her chin.

'Tears?' he questioned gently.

It was the gentleness that was her undoing and she had to bite at her lips to still their trembling. 'Why couldn't you have just left me alone, as I asked?' she choked desolately. 'Was it so important to prove I was no different from any of your other easy conquests?'

'Oh, God, is that what you think?' Ford gave an incredulous shake of his head. Then, leaning over her, he asked urgently, 'Gayna, do you know *why* I flew down to Adelaide today?'

'Because you had business to attend to down here, I suppose,' she whispered, some subtle shading in his voice making her eye him warily.

A wry smile tilted his mouth to one side. 'Mmm, I guess you could say that. Personal business . . . with an aggravating, captivating, little redhead who refuses to stay around long enough for me to tell her how much I want her, or how much I love her!' he revealed hoarsely.

It was in confusion that Gayna caught her bottom lip between her teeth now. 'You love *me*?' she sought confirmation nervously.

'I love *you*,' he repeated deeply.

'A-as well as Felicity and all th-the others?' she faltered.

With a groan he caught her to him tightly. 'Oh, sweetheart, there are no others . . . only you! It's you I love, you I want to marry, you I want to be the mother of my children!' Tipping her head back, he brushed his lips tenderly against hers. 'What more can I say to convince you?'

Gayna's eyes clung to his anguishedly. 'I want to believe you, but I—but I can't! My father . . .'

'Your father, if you'll pardon me for saying so, was a callous, irresponsible bastard I would dearly enjoy having five minutes alone with in order to repay him for the warped impression of men his desertion provided his daughter with!' he ground out savagely. Then his mood lightened as he gave a rueful smile. 'And having got that off my chest, I now want you to tell me something, sweetheart.'

'Such as?' apprehensively.

'Such as why you *wanted* to believe I loved you, even though you said you couldn't believe it.'

'I—why . . .' Unable to hold his intent gaze any longer, Gayna flushed selfconsciously and lowered hers. Even now, she found it difficult to admit to herself. 'You know why,' she murmured almost inaudibly, and in an agony of shyness.

'Do I?' he countered laconically.

'Anyway, three days isn't long enough to . . .' she then started to deny, but a finger laid across her lips prevented her from continuing.

'Uh-uh, I had enough of that concerning Therese and Snow,' he drawled wryly. The finger which had silenced her now began to feather lightly along her jawline. 'Don't you think your future husband is entitled to know how you feel about him?'

At that, her eyes couldn't reach his quickly enough. 'I haven't said I would marry you yet,' she protested.

'You'll have to,' he advised with such a teasing grin breaking over his face that Gayna's pulse raced chaotically. 'How else are you going to have my children?'

Gayna felt like laughing and crying at the same time, and even though she did a little of each, the former at least succeeded in dispelling some of her constraint.

'Oh, Ford, I do love you! I really do,' she was finally able to confess as she impulsively threw her arms around his neck. 'It was just that . . .'

'I know, sweetheart, I know,' he interrupted, smoothing a hand comfortingly over her shining hair. 'You've always been violently opposed to saying that to any man.'

'I didn't intend anyone to ever have a chance of walking out on me like my father did on my mother,' she owned pensively.

His arms tightened about her convulsively. 'And now no one ever will! Because you are going to marry me, aren't you, Gayna?'

Her, considering marriage? It seemed incredible somehow, and yet the two willing nods she gave in response were very credible—as was the teasing glint that appeared in her emerald eyes when she quoted back at him, 'How else am I going to have your children?'

Ford's mouth found hers unerringly, possessively, and arousing both their desires to such an extent that it was only with the greatest difficulty, and reluctance, that he eventually managed to pull away.

'Hell!' He shook his head ruefully, incredulously, his voice heavy with lingering passion. 'Much more of this and I can see us conceiving the first of those children this afternoon! I think I must want you too much, my love, and not seeing you for these last two weeks hasn't helped any either.' He gave a wry half laugh. 'Ever since you left I haven't been able to get you out of my thoughts, and I've snapped so many people's heads off in my frustration that I think they were all relieved to see me depart yesterday.'

'I couldn't think of anything else but you either. I tried . . . but I wasn't successful,' Gayna disclosed selfconsciously in return. 'Although, as I recall,' with a pouted moue, 'at the time you didn't appear very sorry to see me leave. In fact, you preferred to take Felicity with you to Oroya Park rather than fly Alwyn and me to Darwin.'

'Mmm, because I was as mad as hell with you for wanting to leave, and even more infuriated with myself for *not* wanting you to,' he smiled crookedly. 'Believe me, I hadn't intended falling in love with a green-eyed, redheaded little witch whose only wish was to part her mother from my father, any more than you planned to fall in love with me. It just became something over which I found I had absolutely no control, and two weeks was as much as I could take without you.'

Gayna touched her even white teeth to her lower lip doubtfully. 'You're not sorry now, though, are you?'

'I wouldn't have it any other way!' His answer was too tenderly voiced to be disputed. 'Would you?'

'Oh, no!' she sighed just as convincingly, then followed it with a helpless laugh. 'I never realised it before, but I think I must be as impetuous as Mum in some things, after all, because I certainly never meant to fall in love—ever—let alone in just three days.' Her eyes narrowed with mock-indignation. 'And especially not with someone who was so damned rude when I met him that my hand just itched to slap him!'

'I know the feeling,' he retaliated with an impenitent grin. 'There were times when I was hard put to it not to raise a hand to you too, sweetheart. Only mine was wanting to punish a completely different section of your anatomy.'

'Oh! How barbaric,' she endeavoured to remonstrate aloofly, but ended by laughing instead. 'Well, at least you partly succeeded by letting me fall on my seat in the dirt that day at the valley. So what I want to know now is, when do I get my chance at you?' Her eyes sparkled with impish anticipation.

'You've already had it,' he claimed drily.

'When? I don't remember.'

'The afternoon I met you at the airport,' he supplied indolently. 'The instructions Therese gave me that day were just to look for the most beautiful girl there, and that would be her daughter. Naturally, I immediately thought, "Oh, yeah, there speaks a doting mother if ever I've heard one".'

'And?' Gayna prompted, half curious, half amused.

His firm, sensuous mouth took on a wry curve. 'She was right! I walked in the door, took one look at you, and felt as if I'd just been hit with a sledgehammer.' Drawing in a deep breath, he released it slowly. 'You, my love, were definitely not what I'd been expecting, and nor was I prepared for the effect you had on me!'

'So you purposely kept me waiting while you casually chatted with those men . . . and a clinging blonde!'

'I needed time to recuperate from the shock of discovering that Therese's suspicious daughter, who had so many odious insinuations to make, didn't only annoy me, she interested me as well! But as for the clinging blonde . . .' he went on immediately, his deep blue eyes smiling reassuringly into hers 'she happens to be one of my many cousins, nothing more.'

'She didn't look at you in a very cousinly manner,' Gayna couldn't help recalling.

Ford's mouth tilted wryly. 'At the moment she unfortunately seems to be going through that stage where she's infatuated with almost anything in pants.'

'Well, I'll say one thing for her,' she dimpled roguishly, drawing his head down to hers. 'She's got good taste.'

A remark that wasn't to be unrewarded and had his lips closing over hers in a hungry demand she was only too willing to satisfy.

'So what do you think of Therese and Snow getting married on such short acquaintance now?' he murmured thickly much later.

Knowing Ford's and her love had blossomed even

faster, what could she say? 'Only that I don't know what took them so long,' she smiled adoringly, mistily, upwards.

'Oh, God, I love you!' he groaned. 'It's going to be purgatory leaving here and going back to the hotel tonight.'

Gayna's expression turned to one of surprise. 'But there's no need for you to do that. We have two bedrooms here.'

'Mmm.' He appeared to give the matter some thought. Some rueful thought. 'But what's the likelihood of them *both* being used if I did stay, do you think?'

From beneath the curling length of her lashes, Gayna sent him a bewitching glance. 'Very little . . . I hope,' she owned with enchanting honesty.

Masquerade
Historical Romances

Intrigue excitement romance

PROXY WEDDING
by Belinda Grey

The Lady Gida Rune vows never to see Sir Adam de Clancy
again. Soon, however, the rebellious Gida is forced to admit
that marriage – even to Sir Adam – is preferable to the
alternative of being banished to a nunnery,

BRIDAL PATH
by Patricia Ormsby

The new Lord Rotherham desperately needs to produce an
heir to gain his rightful inheritance, for his grandfather has left a
fortune to whichever of his grandsons first has a son. This is one
race his Lordship's new bride, Julienne-Eve, is determined to
help him to win!

Look out for these titles in your local paperback shop from
11th June 1982

Romance

Next month's romances from Mills & Boon

Each month, you can choose from a world of variety in romance with Mills & Boon. These are the new titles to look out for next month.

FORGOTTEN LOVER Carole Mortimer
LATE HARVEST Yvonne Whittal
STARTING OVER Lynsey Stevens
BROKEN RHAPSODY Margaret Way
BLIND MAN'S BUFF Victoria Gordon
LESSON IN LOVE Claudia Jameson
MIDNIGHT LOVER Charlotte Lamb
STORM CYCLE Margaret Pargeter
PACIFIC PRETENCE Daphne Clair
WILDFIRE ENCOUNTER Helen Bianchin
THE OTHER BROTHER Jessica Steele
THE MAGNOLIA SIEGE Pamela Pope

Buy them from your usual paperback stockist, or write to: Mills & Boon Reader Service, P.O. Box 236, Thornton Rd, Croydon, Surrey CR9 3RU, England. Readers in South Africa write to: Mills & Boon Reader Service of Southern Africa, Private Bag X3010, Randburg, 2125.

Mills & Boon
the rose of romance

ROMANCE

Variety is the spice of romance

Each month, Mills & Boon publish new romances. New stories about people falling in love. A world of variety in romance – from the best writers in the romantic world. Choose from these titles in June.

DIAMOND CUT DIAMOND Jane Donnelly
RED ROSE FOR LOVE Carole Mortimer
VALLEY OF LAGOONS Kerry Allyne
A GIRL TO LOVE Betty Neels
BITTER-SWEET WATERS Yvonne Whittal
AN OLD PASSION Robyn Donald
WAITING Karen van der Zee
MAKEBELIEVE MARRIAGE Flora Kidd
EDGE OF TEMPTATION Anne Mather
THE CAGED TIGER Penny Jordan
THE WINDS OF HEAVEN Margaret Way
THE SLEEPING FIRE Daphne Clair

On sale where you buy paperbacks. If you require further information or have any difficulty obtaining them, write to: Mills & Boon Reader Service, PO Box 236, Thornton Road, Croydon, Surrey CR9 3RU, England.

Mills & Boon
the rose of romance

How to join in a whole new world of romance

It's very easy to subscribe to the Mills & Boon Reader Service. As a regular reader, you can enjoy a whole range of special benefits. Bargain offers. Big cash savings. Your own free Reader Service newsletter, packed with knitting patterns, recipes, competitions, and exclusive book offers.

We send you the very latest titles each month, postage and packing free – no hidden extra charges. There's absolutely no commitment – you receive books for only as long as you want.

We'll send you details. Simply send the coupon – or drop us a line for details about the Mills & Boon Reader Service Subscription Scheme.

Post to: Mills & Boon Reader Service, P.O. Box 236, Thornton Road, Croydon, Surrey CR9 3RU, England.
*Please note: READERS IN SOUTH AFRICA please write to: Mills & Boon Reader Service of Southern Africa, Private Bag X3010, Randburg 2125, S. Africa.

Please send me details of the Mills & Boon Subscription Scheme.

NAME (Mrs/Miss) _____ EP3

ADDRESS _____

_____

COUNTY/COUNTRY _____ POST/ZIP CODE _____

BLOCK LETTERS, PLEASE

Mills & Boon
the rose of romance